# The Preserve

# Other Books
# by Brenda M. Spalding

**Florida Wildlife Heroes Series**

The Alligator Dance
The Turtle Thieves
The Snake Traders
The Preserve

**The Green Lady Inn Mystery Series**

Broken Branches
Whispers in time
Hidden Assets
The Spell Box
The Forgers Palette

Blood Orange
Deadly Bargain
Honey Tree Farm
Bottle Alley

# The Preserve

By

Brenda M. Spalding

Copyright© Brenda Spalding 2025

ISBN: 9798988740681

All rights reserved

This book is a work of fiction.
It was inspired by actual events in the Big Cypress National Preserve, past and future. Any resemblance to actual people, living or dead, is entirely coincidental.

Published by
Heritage Publishing U.S.
Bradenton, FL

# Dedication

To the Seminole and Miccosukee Indian Tribes that call
southern Florida home and to the Gladesmen
that hunt and care for the land.
These people have lived on the preserve and in the
Everglades for hundreds of years. They have raised their
children to respect and honor nature
and the creatures that live there.
The land was theirs when no one wanted it. They were the
stewards who protected a way of life that is now threatened.
God help us all.

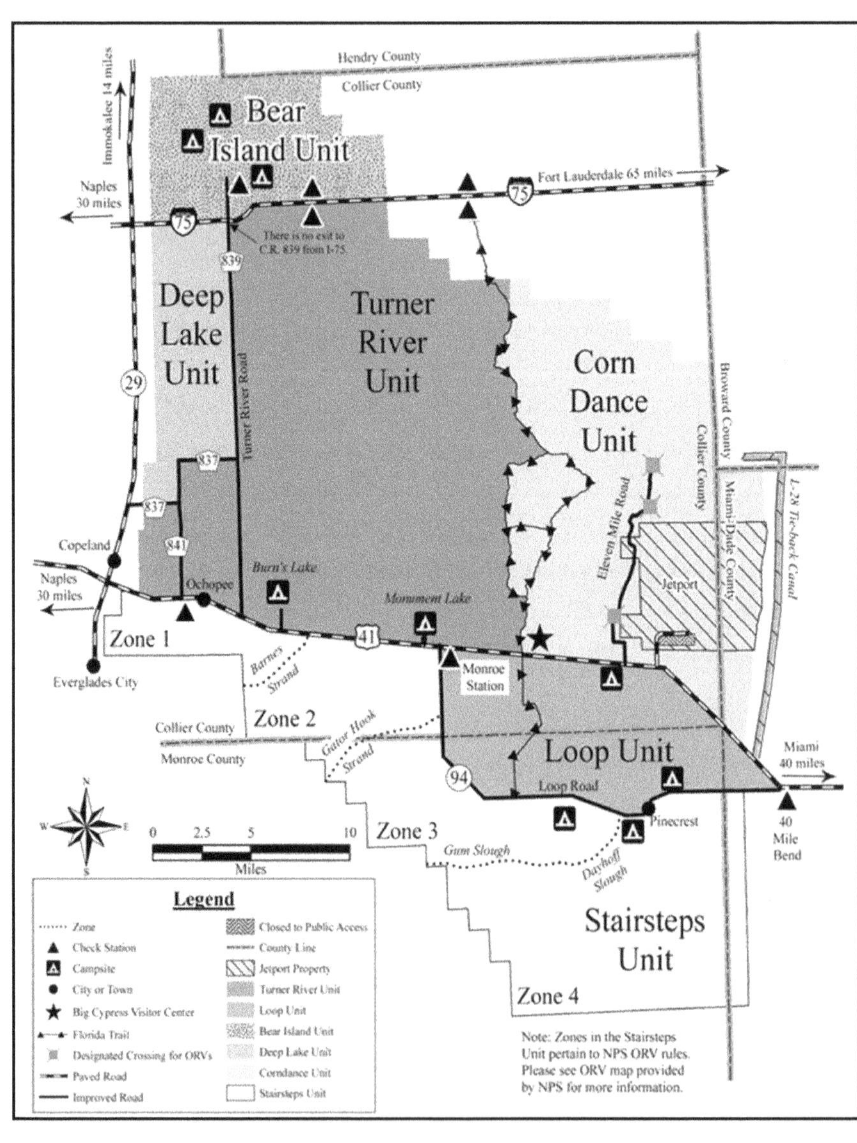

Hendry County
Collier County
Immokalee 14 miles
Bear Island Unit
Naples 30 miles
Fort Lauderdale 65 miles
75
75
There is no exit to C.R. 839 from I-75.
839
Deep Lake Unit
Turner River Unit
Corn Dance Unit
29
Turner River Road
Eleven Mile Road
Broward County
Collier County
Miami-Dade County
L-28 Tieback Canal
837
837
841
Copeland
Burn's Lake
Jetport
Naples 30 miles
Ochopee
Monument Lake
Zone 1
Everglades City
41
Barnes Strand
Monroe Station
Collier County
Monroe County
Zone 2
Gator Hook Strand
Loop Unit
Miami 40 miles
94
Loop Road
Pinecrest
40 Mile Bend
Zone 3
Gum Slough
Dayhoff Slough
Stairsteps Unit
Zone 4
N
W    E
S
0   2.5   5   10
Miles
Legend
Zone
Check Station
Campsite
City or Town
Big Cypress Visitor Center
Florida Trail
Designated Crossing for ORVs
Paved Road
Improved Road
Closed to Public Access
County Line
Jetport Property
Turner River Unit
Loop Unit
Bear Island Unit
Deep Lake Unit
Corndance Unit
Stairsteps Unit
Note: Zones in the Stairsteps Unit pertain to NPS ORV rules. Please see ORV map provided by NPS for more information.

# Chapter One

The ground fog was taking its time lifting, swirling around their legs like invisible serpents as Deputies Seth Grayson and his wife, Deputy Liz Corday, as she was officially known on the job, patrolled Eleven Mile Road, a hiking trail in one of the lesser-used back sections of the Big Cypress National Preserve.

The heavy humidity hung from the Spanish moss and dripped to the ground below.

After their honeymoon in St. Augustine, this was their first day back on duty. They were both happy to return to a routine again, if you could call working as law enforcement officers for the Florida Wildlife Conservation Commission routine.

Seth and Liz had dealt with alligator egg poachers, turtle traffickers, and illegal snake traders on the black market, in addition to their regular duties of checking fishing and hunting licenses and conducting boat safety checks.

Seth's parents had recently moved from the Hillsborough Reservation to the Big Cypress Seminole Reservation. Liz and Seth were fortunate enough to transfer from the Gulf Coast region to Collier County and the Big Cypress National Preserve near the Everglades to be closer to them.

They passed an off-road vehicle (OTV) at the side of the trail.

"I wonder where the owner is?" Liz said.

"Maybe he ran out of gas."

As they walked the trail, a figure materialized from the mist before them along the rugged path. Liz grabbed Seth's arm. "What's that?"

The apparition began to take shape. It was a disheveled man wearing a large backpack. He was obviously in distress, out of breath, and near collapse.

"Oh, thank God. I thought I'd have to drive all the way back to the ranger station. My cell phone is dead." The man said, leaning on his knees to catch his breath. "There's a dead guy back there. At least, I think he's dead. And someone took a shot at me," the man hesitated, "with an arrow."

Liz and Seth looked at each other. A silent thought passed between them. *An arrow, really?*

Seth was a Seminole working in a white man's world but still held to some of the old traditions, as did his parents. He found it hard to believe that one of his own would try and injure anyone in the national preserve, but then anything was possible.

"We're law enforcement officers with the Florida Fish and Wildlife Conservation Commission. First, what's your name?" Seth said.

"I'm Harold Newsom, a biologist from Miami University. I'm studying ghost orchids and the effect of climate change on their environment." Newsom dug in his day pack, pulled out his university credentials, and handed them to Seth.

"What about the man you found?" Liz asked after looking at Newsom's credentials and handing them back to the man.

"He's back there near an oil drilling site. I didn't know that anyone could drill here on the preserve." Newsom said.

"It's a long story. Can you stay here while we go check it out?"

"I'm not going anywhere after finding a dead man and getting an arrow shot at me. My research grant doesn't cover that.

# Chapter Two

The heat and humidity had the officers drenched in sweat as they quickened their pace to find the man, dead or alive. It was the beginning of June, and the wet and stormy season in Florida had arrived.

Rounding a curve on the trail, they saw the drill head a few yards ahead of them.

"What idiot let anyone drill for oil in a national preserve?" Liz said, almost tripping over a rut in the road.

The road was torn up by the large tractor treads used to move the equipment needed to build and run the refinery at Raccoon Point, as well as the oil rigs scattered throughout the preserve.

"Remind me to explain later," Seth answered, pointing to a man half-hidden in the scrub brush of palmetto and massive cypress trees growing by a feeder stream.

An arrow was stuck head high in one of the cypress trees, and growing in the protective shade, a perfect cluster of glowing white ghost orchids appeared above it.

"What's with the arrow?" Liz asked.

"Never mind that for now."

The man was face down and appeared to have been struck by something heavy. His head showed a significant injury, and blood had pooled on the ground, attracting beetles and flying insects.

Ignoring the arrow in the tree, Liz bent to get a closer look, waving the bugs away from her face.

Seth first checked the man's neck for a pulse. He looked at Liz and shook his head, "He's gone."

Searching the man's pockets he found a Texas driver's ID for Adam Hernandez, Houston.

"I wonder what brought him out here?" Seth asked as he came across an ID for the Florida Wildlife Federation in another pocket showing the ID to Liz.

Digging further, Seth found three Miccosukee Resort and Gaming Hotel casino chips. He tossed the chips in his hand, trying to think of possible connections other than Hernandez's fondness for gambling.

Was he meeting someone at the hotel? Did it have to do with the oil business and the oil rights?

Liz was already on the radio calling the finding of the body in. Several agencies would fight for jurisdiction over a dead man found on a national preserve.

When Liz finished the call, Seth showed her the casino chips.

"Guess we're headed to the casino and see who might know our dead guy here," Liz said.

Surveying the area, Seth saw several bootprints leading to and away from the victim. He could read Newsom's prints as they crossed the body and led away down the trail to where he met up with them. They were mixed in with the victim's boot prints coming from the drill head and another partially wiped-out set.

In the heel of one of the sets, a star pattern was barely visible.

There were signs of a confrontation: several overlapping footprints and a large rock stained with blood. The question was who landed the fatal blow.

The arrow in the tree that Newsom reported was a bolt shot from a compound crossbow. It was not the typical Indian arrow Seth was expecting.

Walking the area, Seth found impressions of panther tracks near the water by a fallen tree limb, not just one adult, but an adult with at least one cub.

It was great news for the panther's recovery. It was thought that there were slightly more than 200 panthers left in Florida due to habitat loss. Unfortunately, they were often killed on the roadway trying to find food and territory to live. They were put on the endangered list in 1997.

Several ranchers had banded together to establish a wildlife corridor, allowing panthers and other animals to survive. With encroaching developments like those in Naples, the panthers and bears were being squeezed out of their natural habitats. Encounters with humans were happening more often.

"Come look at this," Seth said, calling Liz over to see the tracks."

"Wow, my first Panther track. I hope I get to see a live one."

"I've never seen a live one either in all the times I've been hunting on the preserve with my father and cousins."

"I wonder if our dead friend over there was killed because of his connection to the drilling or the panthers?" Liz asked.

"I know a few years back they introduced panthers from Texas to strengthen the Florida panthers. Our panthers were on the brink of extinction at that time."

"Our dead guy might have had something to do with that, being as he was from Texas," Seth said.

"Or he could be connected to the oil well."

"We'll have to wait and see. Sheriff Woodson from the Collier County Sheriff's Office is dispatching someone. A park ranger is guiding them out with a forensic team. I wouldn't be surprised to see Special Agent Pat Miller called out on this one, too, since it's federal land."

"Oh, won't that be fun," Liz said, giggling and remembering working with him during their investigation of black-market snake trading in Sarasota.

Seth was less than impressed as the agent had made advances to Liz when they first met.

Seth and Liz sat on part of a tree stump, swatting at flies

and mosquitoes and stamping fire ants off their boots, waiting for someone to show up.

"I wonder how Newsom is doing back there, all alone?" Liz asked. "He looked pretty shook up when we left him."

"It crossed my mind. Why didn't Newsom call for help? Everyone has a cell phone these days."

"Remember he said his phone was dead," Liz said.

"You would think he would have made sure it was charged before venturing to someplace like this."

Liz wondered the same thing, tapping her fingers on her knees. She put that question on the list for the professor.

"He'll be fine," Seth said. "One of the rangers will head him in the right direction. He'll have to give a statement and leave his contact information. We may need to ask him a few more questions later.

In the distance, they heard voices approaching.

A tall, good-looking man in a Stetson appeared around the bend in the trail. "What have you two gotten yourselves into this time?" Special Agent Pat Miller said with a big grin on his face.

The Florida Wildlife Federation was one of seven agencies that could be pulled in to investigate a crime committed in a national park. Soon, state and county police would all be fighting for jurisdiction.

Seth stood and took the man's hands, "You got here fast."

"Nice to see you too."

Liz extended her hand to the agent. "Hey, that just will not do," The man said, grabbing Liz and pulling her into a big bear hug. "That's better." Letting her go. He backed off and gave her a wink.

Agent Miller knew Seth was wary of the agent around his wife, and it would bug him to see him hugging her.

Seth watched, holding his breath and hands on his hips. He hadn't fully trusted the agent around his wife since they worked on a turtle trafficking case a year or so ago. He was just slightly friendly, and Seth was jealous and protective of her. Seth considered Pat a friend and tried to keep an open mind.

The Collier County Sheriff's Department, the forensic team, and the coroner followed up behind them.

Introductions were made, and everyone got down to business.

Seth and Liz took Pat aside and showed him the casino chips, sharing their thoughts on what might be going on.

"You could be right. Hernandez getting murdered might not have anything to do with the proposed new drilling rights or your panthers. You guys fancy a night out at the casino?"

Pat began to walk away with the deputies but suddenly stopped. He took off his Stetson and scratched his head. "You know that name, Adam Hernandez, rings a bell. I think I've run across him somewhere or heard about him. It'll come to me," Pat said, putting his hat on and scowling, trying to think of where and why it was important.

# Chapter Three

They were all exhausted after spending several hours in the heat and humidity at the crime scene. It was the end of May. Memorial Day was approaching, and already the temperature was in the high eighties. The weather channels were warning of hurricanes to come and blasting out to prepare now.

Seth invited Agent Miller to stay at their house on the outskirts of the small town of Immokalee.

"This is different from your place in Sarasota," Pat said as they drove up to the small one-story house in desperate need of repair. The roof was sagging, shutters were falling off, and paint was missing from all sides.

The only thing that was the same was almost getting bowled over by the greeting the agent got from their dog, Nickosi. The big dog seemed to remember Pat and wiggled and wagged enthusiastically.

Seth got the dog as a small puppy, and he just kept growing. His name was Bear in Seminole, and that's what the big dog resembled. Nickosi was lovable and affectionate, but he had protected and warned them about danger more than once.

"Yeah, well, we only moved in a couple weeks ago. The price was right; it's close to my parents and work. We have a big piece of land to cover down here and no highways to get us there.

Liz started pulling things out of the fridge. "Sorry, it's a cold supper tonight. I have some leftover chicken, and I'll throw together a salad. Finding a dead body was not in my plan for today."

"That's OK, Liz. Whatever you have will be fine. We can pick up some groceries tomorrow." Pat grinned.

Nickosi had his huge head across Pat's knee. "Seth, you got a grill out back yet?"

"One of the first things I bought." Seth laughed.

"Great, steaks tomorrow night before we hit the casino."

Sitting down to a quiet meal and catching up was fun until Liz began to yawn. "Oh, sorry, but it's been a long day. Shall we toss for who gets to shower first?"

Seth stood, "I'll let Nickosi out. You two argue over who goes first. I'll take what's left of the hot water."

"Hey, before that. Tell me, what's with the oil drilling in the preserve?" Liz said as she cleared the few dishes from the table.

Pat leaned back in his chair. "Seth, you're closer to this issue than I am."

Seth took a breath, ran his fingers through his raven-black hair, and dug deep to remember how it all came about.

He explained as best he could, watching Nickosi from the doorway.

"The federal government bought the surface rights when the preserve was formed in 1974, about 729,000 acres. They failed to buy the mineral rights. A Texas oil company bought those rights and started drilling. The company continues to acquire more land from the preserve for drilling purposes.

Several environmental groups and the Miccosukee tribe, as well as the Seminoles, have been trying to stop the drilling for decades."

"Can't the federal government repurchase the mineral rights now?" Liz asked.

"I'd have to do some more research. It would cost millions of dollars, and the oil company is leasing the land from the owners who have bargained hard over the price, and the government can't or will not come up with the money."

Pat and Seth both shook their heads. Pat said, "It's a bad situation. The oil company is getting rich while destroying the land. Their trucks are big and heavy, leaving massive fifteen-foot-wide deep tracks, tearing up the vegetation, and we can't do anything about it because the oil company owns the mineral rights."

With a dish towel in hand, Liz said, "That doesn't make any sense."

"Whoever made the deal first didn't think it through with the landowners. They might not have been aware of surface and mineral rights. The landowner basically sold the land twice."

Liz yawned again, "That's a lot to take in. Pat, I'm taking my shower and heading to bed. Seth, don't stay up all night talking."

"I won't. I want to call the Sheriff's office and find out what they found in forensics first thing in the morning."

Liz kissed Seth goodnight with Pat smiling, "Where's mine?"

Seth laughed, "Get your own girl. This one's taken." And he meant it.

# Chapter Four

Nickosi woke everyone up, barking furiously at the door. A Collier County Sheriff's car was in the drive, and two deputies were getting out.

Seth quickly pulled on a pair of jeans and followed Agent Miller to greet the deputies.

"Hey, Officer Grayson, Agent Miller," a stout man with a gray mustache said, extending his hand. "I'm Sheriff Woodson, and this is Deputy Franklin. I understand you were on the scene yesterday when the body of Adam Hernandez was discovered. We received the coroner's report today and thought you might be interested."

"Come on in. We can get some coffee going." Seth said.

Pat held Nickosi back to let the deputies in. The dog wanted to greet the strangers.

Deputy Franklin fell to her knees and embraced Nickosi, "Oh, aren't you a big love," the young female deputy said as she almost disappeared in the fur of the big animal. Nickosi grinned with the attention, flopping onto his back for a belly rub.

Officer Franklin was a thirty-two-year-old attractive redhead who had been on the job for ten years. She had worked her way up and was Woodson's right hand in a lot of things. Studying Criminal Justice at the University of Miami, she aspired to advance in her career and succeed Woodson when he retired in a couple years.

Franklin sometimes thought people didn't take her seriously

because of her appearance and being a woman.

"Franklin, quit playing with that dog and act like a deputy. Woodson liked Deputy Janice Franklin in a father-daughter way. He saw her potential and wanted her to succeed.

Liz entered the room, greeted the deputies, and began setting up for coffee. "I'm surprised the forensic report came through so fast."

"It surprised us, too. Someone above my pay grade must be pushing the paperwork through." The Sheriff said.

"I haven't introduced myself yet." Pat held his hand out to the Sheriff. "I'm Special Agent Pat Miller. I'm assigned to the Department of the Interior when there is something like this on federal land. I'm not going to argue jurisdiction. I'm an observer and an advisor."

"Nice to know we have that covered."

Pat shook hands with Deputy Franklin, lingering a touch longer than necessary.

"What did the report say?" Liz said, handing out steaming mugs of coffee.

"Our dead man had been in a fight sometime before his death. There were bruises on his face and hands that had begun to heal. He had a knife wound on his left side. It wasn't deep, just a slice, but it would have hurt." Woodson spread some photos out on the table.

"The knock on his head is what killed him. It fractured his skull and caused significant brain damage. The coroner thinks he was alive for some time after he was hit, but his outcome was not good either way."

"Do you think he was alive when Newsom found him?" Liz asked.

"I don't think the doc could tell," Pat said.

The Sheriff stood to leave, "Thanks for the coffee, but we have to get going."

"I found some casino chips in his pockets. We plan on going to the casino and nose around a bit. I'll let you know if we find out anything."

"I'd appreciate it."

Seth and Pat walked the Sheriff and the young deputy out, followed closely by Nickosi, who decided to check out the water oak on the side of the house.

After the police had pulled away, Pat surveyed Seth's little house. "This place sure needs a lot of work. Are you sure you're up to it?"

"I've got hidden skills and many relatives to lend a hand if I get stuck. I'll even let you swing a hammer when you're around."

"Oh, jeez, thanks. So long as a meal is thrown in once in a while, you have a deal."

# Chapter Five

Agent Miller took off the next morning, leaving Seth and Liz alone while he attended some other business.

Seth worked on his house, removing the worn shutters and piling them in the backyard.

He called his father at lunchtime, "Hey, Dad, I'm off this weekend. Are you and the cousins up for helping me with a little DIY on my place? I'll throw in some burgers and beer."

"You know your mother and some of the women are going to want to come and make a big deal out of it," Andres Grayson laughed.

Seth's father believed in the old Seminole ways but had come to accept Seth's life choices. He wanted his son to live on the reservation but had to understand that Seth did not.

His mother loved her son and tried to help her husband understand that the world they grew up in was changing.

Seth grew up on the Hillsborough Seminole Reservation in Tampa. He went to college and never went back to Live on the reservation.

After meeting Liz while working on an alligator egg poaching problem in the Sarasota area he decided to become a Florida Wildlife Officer and have been together ever since.

"Liz would love a family gathering. She plans to paint the back bedroom. Don't be surprised if mom ends up with a paintbrush in her hands."

Andres thought for a moment, "What exactly do you have in mind for me and the cousins?"

"I want to have the house painted. It will go quickly the more people I have to help."

Andres chuckled, "You better have plenty of beer on ice and expect some of us to stay over."

Seth didn't mind because he didn't want anyone driving under the influence, and besides, it would be fun to have everyone together at his new house. They talked a bit more to catch up on the family gossip before hanging up.

Liz was in the back bedroom patching holes in the wall and sanding rough places, getting ready for painting.

Seth came up and encircled her with his arms. She smelled of caulking and sweat. It didn't stop him from kissing her neck.

"I talked to my Dad, and he'll see about coming over to help paint the house on the weekend. He thinks my mom will come over, too."

What he didn't tell her was that it was going to be a full-scale family gathering. He didn't want to stress her out.

Seth looked at his watch, "I wonder what Pat has gotten up to? But since we're alone," Seth said with a cocky grin gathering a slightly sweaty Liz in his arms. "Maybe we can jump in the shower and have some play time together."

Liz dropped her head on his chest before pushing him away, "Race you," she said, throwing down the tool she had in her hand and running down the hall, tossing off her clothes as she went.

Seth jumped over Nickosi and barely reached the bathroom before Liz slipped into the shower.

"No fair, you cheated," Seth said, stripping quickly to join her.

# Chapter Six

Liz stepped into the kitchen, towel-drying her damp, sandy brown hair.

Seth came up behind her, nuzzling her neck some more. "Mmm, you smell good now."

"That was fun," Liz said.

"Did I miss something?" Agent Miller said, coming in the door and carrying a large white box with a fancy French name.

Liz turned scarlet, imagining what the agent might be thinking.

"What have you got there?" Seth said.

"Since we are going to the casino tonight, I thought I'd get a little something for Liz to wear. It's a treat for both of you. Going out in khakis and wearing a Glock will not do tonight."

Pat opened the box to reveal a stunning midnight blue cocktail dress. He held it up, and the shimmering fabric caught the light.

Liz was speechless with emotion. It was a long time since she had seen something so lovely. Dainty sequins danced in the bodice and rimmed the waist. The skirt flowed like rippling water.

"Pat, this is too much," Liz said, her eyes misting.

"Yeah, it really is too much," Seth said, his jealousy rising. He should be buying his wife pretty things, not another mans.

"It's part of our cover. The government is paying for it. We'll get more answers if we blend in rather than go in as law enforcement."

Seth could see the sense of that, but the agent was the only man who had ever given him this crazy possessive feeling over Liz. Trying to shake it off, he watched Liz smiling as she swirled around the small kitchen, holding the stunning dress in front of her.

"But I don't have any shoes. I don't think this dress goes with my hiking boots," Liz said.

"Got that covered," Pat said, bringing a pair of silver strappy heels from the bottom of the box.

"Oh God, I haven't worn heels in years."

Seth came up behind her and put his arms around her, "I'll be there to steady you. You are going to look fantastic." Seth wanted to show Pat that Liz was his.

"Let's get this show on the road. We should be there before it gets too crowded." Pat said. Shopping for the dress had put the steaks he had planned off the menu.

Liz prepared a quick meal of sandwiches while the men dressed. Then, it was her turn to dress. She almost didn't recognize herself when she turned to look in the mirror.

"You ready for this," Liz called before entering the kitchen.

Seth was almost speechless as he looked at his wife. "You look amazing." He had never seen her dressed up like this before. He vowed to make it happen more often for both of them.

Pat could only shake his head. And he thought to himself, *I wish I'd found you first.*

Sensing Pat's thought, Seth kissed Liz gently and took her hand in his. "You ready to wow everyone at the casino?"

"Yeah, let's go," Liz said, shaking in her new heels, praying she wouldn't fall off them.

# Chapter Seven

The Miccosukee Resort and Gaming Casino was in full swing when they arrived. It was not overly crowded, but the slot machines were busy and noisy.

Several men, and women too, turned their heads as the deputies walked by.

Pat figured the cocktail bar would be the best place to ask about Hernandez. "I'll start at the bar," he handed Seth and Liz a couple hundred dollars. "You two go to the cashier cage and get some chips to play the tables. Tell the cashier that Adam Hernandez told you about the casino. Ask if he has been in lately."

"I'll see if she knows what tables he liked to play," Liz said.

"Good thinking."

Pat went in one direction, and Seth and Liz went to find the cashier's cage.

They found it tucked away in a corner guarded by armed Miccosukee Tribe members: three outside and two inside the cage.

The guards looked Seth and Liz over as they approached. It was not often a Seminole came to the casino.

Liz put the money Pat had given them through the window, "Hi, can we have some chips, please?"

The young lady looked up as if Liz were from another planet. "What denomination do you want?" she said, rolling her eyes.

"I don't know. Whatever you suggest. Adam Hernandez told us

about this place and said it was great. Have you seen him tonight?"

That seemed to soften the woman up. "He's usually here most nights. He likes to play blackjack and is always on Monica's table."

Liz read the woman's name tag and said, "Thanks, Kiera. I'll try that. Being in a casino is all new to me."

"Try not to lose that dress. It would be a shame." Kiera said and winked.

Liz gathered the chips and turned to look for the blackjack table.

"You ever play blackjack?" Liz asked Seth. She was nervous about standing out and blowing their cover.

"I know the basics, but that's about it. Let's try and find Monica's table."

They walked around the blackjack tables, reading the dealers' name tags, until they found the one they were looking for.

# Chapter Eight

S eth and Liz sat at her table. Monica was dealing with two other players.

"Evening, folks, welcome," Monica said with a smile.

"Thanks. Adam Hernandez recommended this place and said you were the best dealer here." Seth said, watching Monica's reaction."

The dealer paused mid-throw, "How do you know Adam?"

"We came across him in the preserve," Liz said.

"Hey, lady, how about dealing some cards?" a gruff man with a New York accent said.

Monica dealt a few hands. Liz and Seth lost some and won a couple. The two men moved on after losing more than they won.

"Monica, we need to talk. Can you take a break so we can go to some quiet place?" Liz said.

Right away, Monica knew something terrible had happened to Adam. She signaled to the pit boss for a break, and he sent someone to take her place.

The young woman led them to a lounge area and back table where they would not be disturbed.

"It's bad, isn't it?" Monica said.

"Like I said, we came across Adam in the Big Cypress Preserve. Seth and I are Florida Wildlife Commission Deputies. Adam's body was discovered on a back trail. He'd been killed." Liz stopped while

Monica pulled herself together, handing her a cocktail napkin for her tears.

"I knew something would happen. My husband Lucus saw us here a few nights ago. He and Adam had a terrible fight in the parking lot. The security guards stepped in to break it up."

Liz watched a tear escape and rolled down Monica's cheek. "I'm guessing you had feelings for Adam."

"Yeah, he was sweet. We discussed his work with the panthers and his desire to help the animals. He loved the outdoors and nature. He talked about his family in Texas, the horses on the ranch, going camping and fishing with his dad."

Seth got up and walked away, "I'll find Pat."

"Do you know what Adam was doing on the preserve?" Liz said.

"He said he was setting up trail cameras to track the panthers. There was a female with cubs that he wanted to keep an eye on. He'd seen her tracks but never saw her with the cubs. It was his dream to catch her on one of his cameras."

"Thanks for talking with me, Monica. I'm sorry for your loss." Liz said, getting up from the table. "You better get back. One more question. Is your husband Miccosukee?"

"Yes, why?" Monica said.

"It might not mean anything, but there was an arrow about head height in the tree where we found Adam's body."

Monica dropped her head, crying as she bolted for the ladies room.

"Well, I see you've had an interesting conversation," Seth said, watching Monica's retreat as he returned with Pat.

"Let's go home. I'll tell you all about it." Liz said.

# Chapter Nine

Liz sat curled up on the couch, leaning against Seth as she tried to remember all that Monica had told her.

"What bothers me is, if Adam Hernandez was putting up trail cameras, where are they? He would need a pack to carry them in, right? We didn't find a backpack or any kind of carry-all at the scene." Liz said, swirling her glass of red wine before taking a sip.

"I didn't think of that," Seth answered, kissing the top of Liz's head. "The only one with a pack was Newsom, and it seemed rather large for such a small man, now that I think of it."

"I guess whoever shot the arrow could have taken it," Pat said, yawning loudly.

"I think we have three suspects," Liz chimed in, drinking the last of her wine.

"How do you figure three?" Pat yawned again. The drinks he consumed at the casino bar caught up with him, and his brain was foggy. He needed some sleep. The agent hadn't stopped since he arrived from D.C. two days before.

"I think we have to consider Monica's husband, Lucas Osceola. Then, there is Dr. Newsom and the backpack. The third one is the unknown shooter of the arrow. I wonder about that. Of course, Monica's husband could have shot the arrow, and Dr. Newsom killed Hernandez," Liz said, finishing her wine. "I'm too tired to think anymore. Let's pick this up in the morning."

Pat rubbed his hands over his face, "I'm going to check out Hernandez and his connection to the Florida Wildlife Federation. I'll make some phone calls in the morning. If he was setting out cameras, we need to find them. At the very least, they are federal property."

The agent stood and stumbled his way back to his room, mumbling a good night.

Seth picked up the empty glasses and carried them to the sink. "We have patrol in the morning. No off-trail vehicles (OTVs) are allowed on the trails from June 2 to August 3. We have to get out there and get the signs posted."

"I hope that doesn't mean we get to walk for two months in the summer heat." Liz groaned.

Seth came and threw his arms around her, "No, sweetheart, we can still ride."

Liz leaned her head into Seth's chest. She looked at his eyes and pleaded, "I'm tired. Carry me." She giggled.

"Only if you carry me first."

# Chapter Ten

The trail Seth and Liz followed led to Burns Lake Campgrounds. Some called it Burns Island. The trail encircled the lake, with several designated camping spots. The maximum stay was ten days. The top of the trail led to backcountry campgrounds. You had to be pretty dedicated as that area was very primitive with no facilities.

They passed the RV parking section, waving to some of the visitors sitting outside their units. Liz had Seth stop and check fishing licenses and boat registrations while she checked for life preservers and fire extinguishers.

"That was fun," Liz said, hopping on the four-wheeler behind Seth.

"You're such a people person," Seth said.

"I like people to know that we are doing our job to protect them and not just here to hassle them."

It was afternoon, and the heat and humidity were oppressive even at the end of May. They passed the turnoff for the backcountry and arrived at the next campground.

A young family was anxiously running around their campsite. Supplies were scattered everywhere: burger wrappers, pizza boxes, and other food containers. One of the tents was torn to pieces.

Seth jumped off, asking, "What happened here?"

The dad said, "It was a bear. I've never been so scared in my life. We heard it tearing into the food containers. I got my wife and the kids back in the car and watched. We couldn't do anything. It even attacked the tent where the kids had been sleeping."

Seth and Liz walked around the site. Bear tracks were everywhere.

Liz looked into the torn tent. She came back out with a couple empty cheese puff packages.

"I'll need to make a report. Can I see your ID?" Seth said.

While Seth talked to the husband, Liz spoke to the wife. "I'm Deputy Liz Corday. What's your name?"

"Linda Thomson, Lyn, please," the wife said.

"How was your food stored? Lyn," Liz asked.

"We had it in plastic containers near the campfire. Jason cooked some burgers for supper, and we cleaned up and put everything away. I washed the pan and the utensils and put the paper plates in the trash. We thought we did everything right."

Liz picked up a plastic lid and showed it to Lyn.

"This is what bear claws do to plastic," Liz said, showing Lyn the shredded top that now looked like a cheese grater. "You must put all food-related items in a metal container, preferably in the car."

"This was our first time camping and probably our last. We're down from Georgia, exploring Florida. My husband Jason, son Kevin, and daughter Jennifer."

Seth and Jason joined them. Everything checks out. "We'll help you clean up. You've had quite an experience."

Their little girl, Jennifer, came over with her hands behind her back. "Can I give you something?" she said with a sweet smile.

Liz knelt to the child's level, "OK, what do you have?" Liz was expecting a shell or a butterfly.

"Show the deputy what you have," Lyn said.

"I found this in a tree. Isn't it pretty?"

Liz almost fell over. The child had a perfect ghost orchid in her small hand.

Seth came up behind and touched Liz's shoulder, "I'm afraid we have a little problem here. That's a ghost orchid, and they are protected. You are not allowed to pick them.

The little girl looked at Seth and Liz and then at the flower in her hand. Tears gathered in the child's eyes and dripped down her sun-kissed cheeks.

"Oh, you didn't know, but now you do," Liz said, taking the child in her arms. "I didn't mean to make you cry. Some plants, flowers, and even animals are rare and need to be protected, allowing them to live and grow where they belong. You just happened to find one."

"I can't put it back," Jennifer said, cringing. "I'm so sorry."

"Maybe when you get home, you can look up the ghost orchid on your computer and learn all about them."

The campsite was clean, and all the Thompson's gear was stowed back in their SUV. They would have an adventure to tell folks when they go home to Georgia.

"We have to move on. I hope the rest of your trip goes better." "Where are you headed from here?" Seth asked.

Mr. Thompson adjusted his canvas sun hat and said, "We're going to Marathon in the Keys. We have a campsite reserved for two days down there. After that, it's back up to Georgia. Please tell me there are no bears in the Keys."

Seth chuckled, "No, no bears, but still keep all your food as if there were. Raccoons and other animals would love to have a meal at your expense.

Liz tugged on Seth's sleeve and nodded for them to go.

"Good luck and safe travels," Seth said, waving to the family.

"If we hurry, we have time to chase down Lucas Oceola and see what he has to say for himself."

# Chapter Eleven

Their first stop was the casino to get an address for Monica and her husband, Lucas Osceola. The office manager was not very welcoming.

"We usually don't give out that information to anyone," The manager said, standing behind his desk with his hands on his hips, glaring at Seth and Liz. The manager was a short, stout, older Miccosukee man. He wasn't too sure where he stood with law enforcement asking for personal information.

"As I explained," Seth said, "We are Law Enforcement deputies with the Florida Fish and Wildlife Commission and only need to ask him a couple questions about an incident in the preserve a couple days ago. He might not be involved at all, and we need to eliminate him from our inquiries."

That seemed to soften the manager's attitude. "Well, if that's all you want, I guess it's OK. Monica is a good worker. Her husband, Lucas, sometimes stirs things up. He's got a jealous streak when it comes to Monica. A few days ago, there was a bust-up in the parking lot with some guy, and security had to step in."

The manager sat and typed on his computer, mumbling to himself. "My office assistant knows where this stuff is, but she's at lunch. I'm lucky I know how to turn this darn thing on."

Seth wandered around the office. There were several pictures of semi-famous people on the walls, primarily sports celebrities from Miami looking to lose a few thousand dollars and get their photos in the papers doing it.

"Here it is," the manager said, handing over a slip of paper with the address on it. "Monica starts her shift in a couple hours. You can probably catch them both home right now."

"Thanks for your help," Liz said and followed Seth out.

Blinking and adjusting her sunglasses from the sun's glare, Liz said, "I hope this place is close. I'm starving."

Seth looked at his schoolgirl-trim wife, "Sometimes I just don't know where you put it all."

# Chapter Twelve

The GPS guided them to a small house not far from the casino. A beat-up Chevy with a flat tire and no plate sat in the overgrown weeds, serving as a driveway at the side of the house. Its paint scorched off and faded by the sun.

Seth knocked on the screen door and listened for the sounds of life inside.

"Yeah, hold your horses. I'm coming." A man yelled from the back of the house. "You better not be selling nothing."

Yanking open the door and talking through the screen, the man shouted, "What the hell do you two want?"

Lucas Osceola stood there barefoot, unshaven in a stained sleeveless t-shirt, rubbing the sleep out of his eyes.

"Mr. Osceola, we're deputies from the Florida Fish and Wildlife Commission and would like to ask you a couple questions about an incident you had with Adam Hernandez," Seth said.

Looking very confused, Lucas said, "What on earth does that have to do with Fish and Wildlife?

Liz was sweating and tried to appeal to the man's better side. "Mr. Osceola, could we please come inside? Maybe have a glass of water. It's sweltering out here, and you're wasting the AC standing here."

The man thought this over, shaking his head, and then opened the door to let them in.

"Is Monica home?" Liz asked.

"No, she's getting some stuff for my supper, and then she's going to work at the casino."

Liz looked sideways at Seth and huffed. Walking in, Liz and Seth discovered an almost tidy living room. Beer cans and an overflowing ashtray littered the scratched and stained wooden coffee table in front of the well-worn couch, facing a giant TV that dominated the small room.

Liz knew that Monica would be the one to clean up the mess. One thing stood out. At one end of the couch, an end table held a lamp and several brochures from Big Cypress National Preserve.

Liz flipped through them and found a well-worn trail map. These were sitting on books about the Florida Everglades. Computer printouts about the ghost orchids and panthers in the preserve were stuffed in the book. Someone had been doing research.

"So, what are you guys here for?" Lucas said, taking his usual place on the couch. The springs groaned as he sat.

"Adam Hernandez was found dead in the preserve the other day. We know you had a confrontation with him at the casino. Did you take it any further and follow him into the preserve to finish the fight?"

"Whoa, I didn't have anything to do with his being dead," Lucas said, standing to defend himself. "You think I killed him?"

"It crossed our minds," Liz said.

"Do you ever go bow hunting in the preserve?" Seth asked.

"Yeah, and sometimes with my rifle. It depends on the season and what I'm after. I do follow the rules."

"An arrow was found in a tree near the body," Seth said.

"Well, then I know for sure it wasn't me."

"How can you be so sure? You said you go hunting with a bow," Liz said, hands on her hips.

Lucas rushed to the other side of the room and ripped open a closet door. He pulled out a canvas bag and unzipped it.

"Here is the bow I hunt with. It's a Barrett Stalker, and I use Headhunter bolts. So, it's not my arrow."

Seth took the bow and was impressed with its compact size and lethal capability.

"Sorry, but we had to ask," Seth said, handing the bow back. "That's a pretty expensive piece of equipment. May I ask how you can afford something like that?"

"I worked for it and saved up. That's how."

Lucas returned the bow to the closet, slamming the door shut.

He had a full head of steam going now. He was a member of the Miccosukee tribe and took pride in it.

"I didn't kill Hernandez. He's not worth the trouble. I've hunted in the preserve all my life. It's those idiots in Washington who are trying to take more of the preserve for a wilderness area. That's who I'm against. The tribes and the Gladesmen are fighting it. If Washington had their way, we would lose access to land we have hunted on and used for generations. They are trying to take our way of life away from us. It's not right."

Lucas paced around in front of the couch. Seth and Liz kept a wary eye on him.

"Did you go to the preserve on Monday or Tuesday after you fought with Adam?" Seth said, moving to stand facing the man to stop him from moving.

Lucas leaned into Seth. "No, I did not. I waited until Monica came home and had a screaming match with her. You can ask the neighbors. I'm sure they heard it all."

Lucas fell to his seat on the couch and popped a beer. "Now, get the hell out of my house."

Closing the screen door behind themselves, Liz and Seth looked at each other. "That was intense," Seth said.

"I'm not sure I believe him. He's aware of the current situation in the preserve and the legislation the government is attempting to pass. He's a lot smarter than he looks." Liz said.

"That's what's bothering me. Why did he bring it up? Lucas might be using that to cover what he's up to. Why the arrow in the tree? If Lucas didn't do it, who did? That seems so out of place."

"My head hurts from trying to figure it out, and I'm starving,"

Liz said. "It's getting late. There's a Mexican restaurant on the corner. Can we get something to eat or a takeout?'

"We can get takeout. It's getting late. Please don't eat it all in the car before we get home. Leave some for me, please."

# Chapter Thirteen

Liz found Seth at the kitchen door, watching Nickosi nosing around the palmettos. They had discussed putting up a fence around the property but couldn't decide on the type they wanted. The old place in Sarasota was located on a seldom-used dirt road, but there was more traffic here. Nickosi was not prone to wandering, but they couldn't trust that something might catch his attention and put him in danger.

Leaning into Seth's side, her head on his shoulder, she said, "What do you want to do today? We can try to find Professor Newsom and ask him some questions."

Seth turned to take Liz in his arms, resting his chin on her head. "I've got a better idea. I want to see my parents. My dad might have some insight into this government plan to make more of the preserve a wilderness."

"I like that idea," Liz said, disengaging from Seth's arms and urging him to sit on the steps beside her. Nickosi came and wriggled himself between them.

"We need more answers," Seth said. "If Hernandez was setting up trail cameras, where did they go? We didn't see any at the crime scene. He was trying to track the panthers. Maybe he caught something else on the cameras that got him killed. I might ask the cousins to look for any trail cameras in the area where we found Hernandez. It will cover more ground that way. They can also look for more panther tracks while they're out there.

Liz thought briefly, "As much as I want to see your parents, we should go and find that professor. Your family will be here over the weekend, and we can talk to all of them about the preserve and the cameras then."

"And that's why I married you, sweetheart," Seth said, planting a kiss on Liz's lips.

Seth's phone rang in his pocket, "Hi Pat, What's up?"

Seth stood to walk while he talked. He put the call on speaker. Liz listened intently to their conversation.

"Hernandez was with the Wildlife Federation, but he got involved with this thing about the government making more of the preserve a wilderness. He was riding the fence and making enemies on both sides. Hernandez wanted to protect the Florida panthers but agreed that the Seminoles and Miccosukees had rights to the land. The oil companies were fighting to keep things as they were so they could keep drilling and even expand operations."

Seth kicked a stone on the path, "Talk about a rock and hard place."

"I'll be back your way over the weekend. You can fill me in on what you have found out. Oh, and say hi to Liz for me." Pat chuckled, knowing it annoyed Seth.

# Chapter Fourteen

Luckily, the University of Miami was located in Coral Gables, just a short distance off Highway 41.

Seth pulled his truck into the lot in front of the administration building and took a breath. He didn't like driving in city traffic.

A blast of heat struck Liz and Seth as they left the air-conditioned truck and headed in to see if they could locate Professor Newsom.

The building was a tremendous relief from the heat of the outside. It smelled of old books and waxed floors.

The receptionist behind the desk appraised Liz and Seth's uniforms. "What can I do for you, officers?"

Liz was surprised by the friendly greeting. Most receptionists she had encountered were bored older ladies trying their best to get in her way.

"We're here to see Professor Newsom. Could you tell us where we might find him?" Liz returned the greeting with her best smile.

The woman raised her reading glasses and flipped files on the computer screen. It took several minutes to retrieve the professor's schedule. "He's in the Gifford Arboretum this morning. He's giving a student lecture." The receptionist handed Liz a campus map and circled the location of the arboretum.

Seth tipped his hat, nodding his thanks. Liz said, "Thank you. This map helps. We've never been here before."

"You're welcome officer. Have a nice day, and enjoy the arboretum while you're here. It's a very nice and interesting place."

Liz read the woman's name badge. "How long have you been working here?"

"Oh my, I've been here fifteen years now. I started volunteering after my husband died. I needed something to do. Harold and I used to come to the arboretum with a picnic when the weather was right. We loved it so much."

"Thanks again, Doris. It was nice meeting you."

# Chapter Fifteen

Liz read from the brochures she picked up as they walked. It was cooler under the trees. The pathways were marked as they made their way to where Professor Newsom was giving his lecture.

"The Arboretum is set on 260 acres, with hundreds of different species of trees, plants, and even butterflies on the grounds. I'd love to come back when we have time to explore, maybe pack a picnic like Doris and Harold used to do," Liz said with a little giggle as she shoulder bumped Seth.

"I knew food had to be involved somehow," Seth laughed. He was always amazed at how Liz could eat so much while keeping her figure. Seth loved her curves, and they were all in the right places.

However, he did notice that she hadn't finished all her burrito yesterday, which was unusual.

They saw a group sitting under a large banyan tree a few more steps ahead. Professor Newsom was giving a lecture on the mythology of the banyan tree.

Liz stopped, pulling Seth down on a nearby bench. Shushing Seth from interrupting, "This is interesting. I want to listen for a few minutes."

"The banyan tree is a type of fig tree," Newsom said. "Several Asian countries have myths and legends surrounding this tree. In Hinduism, it is the resting place for the God Krishna. In Guam, Taotaomona is said to be the location where spirits are believed to guard the banyan trees. Then, in Okinawa, the tree is known as gagumaru and is said to be home to the mythical Kijimuna. There are also similar stories in Vietnam and the Philippines."

The professor looked over his students, noticed the officers, and hesitated. "That will be all for today. I want a five-hundred-word essay on the banyan tree on my desk Monday morning."

The class groaned and dispersed, breaking into groups and returning to their following courses.

Newsom gathered his papers into his oversized briefcase, "What can I do for you today, officers?"

"We were wondering if you saw any trail cameras while you were out looking that day you discovered Hernandez's body?" Seth said.

Newsom rolled his eyes down and to the left, hesitating before answering. "No, why do you ask?" He pretended to search through his briefcase, looking for something.

"Hernandez was tracking a family of panthers for the Wildlife Federation. He had placed some cameras along their route, but they went missing. We found some panther tracks but no cameras. Did you see anyone else when you were out there?"

Liz was wandering between the many aerial roots of the banyan tree. She was thinking about the orchid and the arrow.

"Professor Newsom, was the arrow already in the tree when you saw the orchid?" Liz ran her hands up and down the roots, fascinated by their structure in holding the tree up.

Newsom fumbled for an answer. "No, I saw the orchid and went to get a closer look. I know it's protected." He quickly added. "I had my phone out to take a picture when this arrow came flying over my head. I can tell you it scared the hell out of me."

Liz stopped and stood in front of Newsom. "Let me get this straight. When we first saw you, you were high-tailing it out of there to report finding Henderson's body. But you had a cell phone? You could have called 911. You never mentioned someone shot the arrow at you while you supposedly took a picture of the ghost orchid."

"It didn't work, I couldn't take the picture. The darn phone was out of power. I told you that already." The professor was getting agitated.

Seth rubbed his hand over his chin and paced around. Some things didn't add up here. "Professor Newsom, we may need to talk to you again. Someone was out there and shot that arrow at you. Either they were a terrible shot, or it was a warning. For your safety, please stay out of the preserve for now."

Newsom clutched his well-worn leather briefcase to his chest and nodded, "Oh, I will."

Newsom took off like a scared rabbit.

Heading to the truck, Seth said, "I don't believe everything he's telling us. How about we get Pat to check and maybe get a search warrant? There's something not right there."

A young man stepped out from behind one of the giant oak trees lining the path. "Excuse me, deputies," a tall, slim student carrying an overstuffed backpack said.

Liz stopped, "What can we do for you?"

"I saw you talking to Professor Newsom. I heard he found a dead body in the preserve." The student looked around, nervous that someone might see him talking to the deputies. "He goes there a lot. I probably shouldn't say anything, but I know he's interested in ghost orchids and trying to grow them. He has a greenhouse at his house where he grows orchids. Maybe you should check it out."

The man looked around again, ready to run.

Seth stood in his way, "May we have your name, young man? That might be valuable information."

The student stumbled over his words, "Look, I don't want to get involved. I just thought you might want to check out his greenhouse."

Liz put on her best smile, "We understand and won't bother you if we don't have to. Please, what's your name? Just for our notes."

"My name is Malcolm, Malcolm Fletcher. I'm an environmental ecology major studying for my Ph.D."

"That's wonderful Malcolm. I wish you all the best," Liz said.

They watched Malcolm scurry away down the path.

Liz and Seth looked at each other. "That was strange. Maybe we need to add the greenhouse to Pat's search warrant." Seth said.

Liz was silent for a moment, her head tipped to the side, thinking,

"OK, what's going on in that gorgeous head of yours?"

"The sticker on his backpack, Straight Arrow Archery."

# Chapter Sixteen

S eth returned from Home Depot with his truck loaded with paint and other supplies to find his home invaded by relatives eager to lend a hand.

There were tables laid out in the yard for tools. Ladders were raised against the house, and radios were blasting.

As soon as he turned off the engine, his cousins began to take out the supplies and pass them around. In minutes, his father, Andreas, was barking orders about what would be done and who would do what.

Seth dodged a moving ladder and rushed into the kitchen to check on Liz, only to find her wrist deep in something she was making with his mother.

Several other women, aunts, and in-laws were bustling in the kitchen, setting out food or cooking and stirring on the stove. He ducked his head as a tray passed on its way to the oven and danced around one of his aunts wiping up cornbread.

Liz washed her hands before embracing Seth, "Isn't it wonderful." Liz was breathless with excitement, her face flushed with it. Growing up as an only child, she had not experienced what an entire family gathering was like. Her parents had divorced and gone their separate ways, leaving her to find her own way in life. Liz's father had died several years ago. Her mother was not happy with her choice of career or husband.

"Your mother is teaching me to make, oh, I can't remember what it's called, fluttering her hands, but it will be great. Your aunt Cami is making something with sweet potatoes. There are salads, and someone will fire up the grill for chicken and other stuff later."

Seth kissed his mother, Rowena, on the cheek, "Thanks, mom for all this."

"Your father got me up at dawn to come over here. We called on your cousins, Zachery, Isia, Matthew, and anyone else he could think of. Zackery has been hunting, so who knows what will end up on that BBQ grill. I suspect alligator and python will be there." Rowena said, laughing. "Now get out of here and let the women work." Seth's mother pushed him towards the door.

He could only marvel at how his mother and father had brought the entire family together for him and Liz. He was blessed and thankful to have such wonderful and supportive parents. He knew it was something Liz missed having with her parents.

Special Agent Pat Miller stood on the step as Seth opened the kitchen door.

"I'll take a coffee. It's too early for a beer, and don't you think about putting a paintbrush in my hand," the agent grinned, tipping his Stetson.

Seth brought him into the kitchen, where the women made eyes at the tall, good-looking agent and chatted in their native language, Seminole.

Pat took off his hat and almost blushed at the attention. He distracted the women by making a big deal over the dishes they were preparing, asking for the names of things and a taste.

The women giggled like schoolgirls as Liz handed Pat his coffee and escorted him to the living room, away from his admirers.

"What have you found out, Pat," Seth asked, sitting beside Liz.

"I did some digging, and Adam Hernandez was working for the Florida Wildlife Federation. He recorded the births and deaths of panthers and the cubs in the preserve. He was involved in bringing some of the Texas Panthers to Florida a few years ago. Hernandez was setting up trail cameras in spots where females had been known to cross. He was also working with some groups on the Florida Wildlife Corridor."

Seth leaned forward in his seat, "What did you mean the death of the cubs? I thought the mother panther would protect them."

"I asked that same question. It has to do with the overall population of the panther in general. Some cubs don't make it past the first few weeks. The mother has to leave them to go out and hunt.

"Say a mother has three cubs. She's out hunting, and a male that's not the father comes along. He will kill the cubs. That could be why you only saw tracks of one adult and one cub. The other two were killed. Maybe by a male panther or another predator."

Liz's mouth fell open. "I read something about that. That's like with the African big cats. They will kill cubs that are not theirs so they can mate with the mother and have their cubs."

They were interrupted by Andres, carrying a wet paintbrush in his hand. "Hey Seth, you going to sit there all day while the rest of us do all the work?

"I'm coming," Seth said, pushing himself up. "I want to hear more. Liz can tell you what we learned about Professor Newsom."

"If I stick around, can I have some of what those women are cooking in the kitchen?"

"Only if you work for it," Seth laughed.

"I knew it." Pat groaned.

Andres smirked, handing Pat the paintbrush and guiding him out the door.

# Chapter Seventeen

Andres put Pat to work painting the back porch while he set up the grill.

The cousins, Isia and Matthew, laughed as they unloaded a huge red cooler from the back of an old pickup truck.

Pat stopped painting and wondered what was in the cooler. It was almost noon, and he could use a cold beer right about now.

His eyes popped as he saw one of the young men take out an enormous python and lay it on a table. It had to be at least twelve feet long.

Stomach churning, he watched as the snake was skinned, cleaned, and chopped into pieces, then placed in a bowl with spices.

He should be OK with things like this. He's heard of people eating pythons but never witnessed it before.

Paint from the brush dripped on the floor, but Pat couldn't take his eyes off the men.

Zackery came over and helped to drag a ten-foot gator off the truck's bed.

Andres began to instruct the men on how to butcher the gator properly. They, in turn, argued back that they knew what they were doing. The cousins each claimed the hide, further complicating things.

Pat was fascinated by the exchange and jumped when Seth came up behind him.

"Hey, you're getting more paint on the floor than on the railing."

"Are you guys really going to eat that?" Pat said, pointing with his brush to the table covered with blood and gore.

"Oh, we have chicken and burgers for sissies like you."

"I think I'll stick with a burger. Aw, you haven't ground up a python or something in those burgers, have you?"

"Naw, It's the wrong season for deer burgers," Seth walked away laughing.

Pat was left shaking his head, wondering what he had gotten himself into. Things were much more civilized when he worked with Seth and Liz in Sarasota.

Getting back to painting, he was almost finished when the tantalizing smell of something cooking wafted over from the grill area.

Tables and chairs were set up. The women were bringing their dishes from the kitchen.

Pat hurried to finish the last couple of rails on the porch. He was starving and looking for that cold beer.

He raised his eyes to the sky and said a silent prayer. *Please, God, don't make me eat python.*

Seth came to his rescue, handing him that beer. "Get that down and wash up. There's plenty. I'll save you some python and gator."

Seth walked away, glancing back over his shoulder and laughing at the look of horror on Agent Miller's face.

# Chapter Eighteen

Music played in the background, featuring soft Seminole rhythms mixed with some country, along with voices in English and Seminole, was heard around the tables.

Liz and Pat sat across from Seth, his family to his left. Dishes passed back and forth.

Andres helped Pat to another helping, "You like that one?"

"Yeah, this sauce is terrific. The chicken is perfect," the agent said, taking another mouthful.

Andres winked at Seth. Liz and Seth both tried to hide their snickering laughter. Seth's mother, Rowena, poked her husband in the ribs.

The agent's lips were smeared with Seminole Gold BBQ sauce, and while talking with his mouth full, he said, "What's so funny?"

"You do know you're eating python," Seth said.

Looking down at his half-empty plate, "Well, I'll be. I never thought I'd eat python and like it."

"When you finish eating that snake, Liz and I have to talk to you about what we learned about Professor Newsom."

Pat pushed his plate away, "You just ruined a perfectly good meal by reminding me I was eating a snake. I had enough of snakes with those black-market traders importing poisonous snakes in Sarasota."

Taking fresh beers, they found a quiet spot on the freshly painted back porch. The sun had moved, casting the back of the house in deep shade from a giant oak tree.

With Nickosi at her feet, Liz told the agent what Malcolm Fletcher said about Newsom's greenhouse.

"I think we need a search warrant for that greenhouse and the professor's quarters at the university," Seth said.

"I'll get that started. Should I run a check on this Malcolm Fletcher while I'm at it?" Pat said.

"I think we need to. He had a sticker on his backpack that said Straight Arrow Archery."

"There was something about that kid. He was too willing to help. Almost trying to get the professor in trouble." Seth said.

Liz leaned back in her chair, "Hey, Chief, you up for some archery practice? I can call and see if they're open tomorrow."

"No point telling you two to stay out of trouble is there."

"Who us? Get in trouble? Naw, we're just poking around." Seth said.

"You've tried that before and almost got killed," the agent said.

"Yeah, I know. People are leaving. I'll be back." Seth said. He needed to talk with his parents and thank everyone who had come to help.

His house was painted. The roof was repaired, and everyone enjoyed spending time together as a family and sharing a meal.

He stood in the driveway and watched the cars and pickup trucks pull away. Nickosi nudged his leg. Scratching the big dog's head, he knew he had made the right decision to move closer to his family.

Liz had never had a proper family life and seemed to enjoy his so much. She was bonding with his mother, and Seth was thankful for that.

# Chapter Nineteen

Seth saw his cousins about to pull away and stopped them. He wanted to thank them again for supplying the alligator and the python.

He couldn't help but notice the crossbow hanging on the gunrack in the back of the truck's cab.

"Hey, fellas, thanks for the extra meat today. I appreciate it." Seth said, standing beside the passenger side door."

"That's not a problem, cousin. It's what families do. You have a nice place here, and it's good to have you and Liz close for a change." Isia said, sticking his hand out to shake with Seth.

"I see the crossbow. That's a beauty. Which one of you does that belong to?"

Zackery, sitting behind the wheel, said, "That's mine. I hunt wild pigs with it. You want me to bring you some next time I go out?"

"That would be great. I want to go with you all sometime soon. I also want to ask you about something else if you have a minute.

"Sure, what?"

"I hear the government is trying to make part of the preserve a wilderness area, which would lock out the Seminoles and the Miccosukee from using areas the tribes have used for generations."

Seth could see Zackery's hands tense on the steering wheel.

"That's right. I attend the council meetings between the

Seminole and Miccosukee tribes. You should come and get the whole story."

Matthew and Isia nodded their heads in agreement. "There is no easy solution. The land used to belong to the tribes, and the government took it away," Isia said softly under his breath.

Seth could feel the tensions over the issue.

"No one person should own the land or what lives there. It needs to be protected for future generations," Matthew added.

Zackery put the truck in gear, and Seth barely had time to step out of the way before the cousins sped off.

Seth stood in his driveway, watching the truck disappear down the road. He had a lot of questions for his cousins, but could he ask them, or should he ask them?

He was deep in thought when Liz slid her arms around his waist and kissed his neck. "What's up, Chief?"

"Something I have to ask my father about." He turned and hugged Liz. Over her head, he looked at his newly painted house and sighed. One problem solved.

"I'm hungry. Let's go see if there's any leftovers?" Seth said.

"I don't believe it. That's usually my line." Liz laughed and took Seth's hand to raid the small kitchen.

# Chapter Twenty

Straight Arrow Archery Club was located in a strip mall on the outskirts of Naples. It backed up to an open field with no visible houses. Targets were set up in the field. A line of dense oak and palmetto acted as a barrier for any stray arrows.

Even on a Sunday morning, Seth had to circle the parking lot to find a parking space.

Seth and Liz had decided to try their undercover personalities again. They had used them before to dismantle the illegal turtle trafficking ring.

They walked in and looked around before approaching the reception desk.

One wall featured recurve longbow sets. Liz was surprised by the styles and sizes offered, ranging from beginner children to adult professional hunters.

It moved on to the compound bows, and the prices ranged from under a hundred to thousands.

Next to the checkout, a bookshelf held books and pamphlets on the Everglades and Big Cypress National Preserve. Some were the same as Liz had seen at Monica's house.

A door led to the outdoor archery range, and they could see the targets set up. Students and teachers were ready or waiting for their turn.

"No wonder the parking lot is full," Seth said.

A tall, husky, bearded man wearing a tee shirt with the Straight

Arrow Archery Club logo on the front approached them.

"Can I help you folks find somethin'?"

"We're looking for a new hobby and thought we might try archery," Seth said. He wore jeans and cowboy boots, sporting a tropical shirt with gold chains around his neck.

The man looked him up and down, rubbing his beard.

"You're pretty far off the reservation, aren't you?"

"We can't all live on government handouts and gator tails."

No matter what he did or where he went, Seth was always a Seminole in Florida. His features and raven-black hair gave him away every time. He learned long ago to take pride in his heritage and sometimes use it to his advantage.

The man laughed, his gaze fixed on Liz. "Looks like you got yourself a nice bit of tail right there."

Seth seethed at the remark but didn't show it. He threw his arm around Liz's shoulder. "She can be tricky as a gator when she wants to be too." He winked at the man and laughed.

The man stuck out his huge hand, "The name's Karl."

Seth shook hands. "Yeah, I don't want any sissy bow and arrow thing. I want the real deal." He pointed to a mid-range Barrett Stalker crossbow.

"Yeah, some of those look deadly," Liz said, snapping her chewing gum. She had taken on the persona of a dumb, low-class broad. It had worked in the past.

"That's not for beginners," Karl said.

"It takes arrows, and you shoot with it, right?" Seth said, taking the crossbow off the wall. It was heavier than he expected.

"It takes bolts. They are different than arrows. Heavier and stronger for hunting."

"Maybe I can talk to someone that uses this type of crossbow. You know, I need to get their opinion before I decide." Seth could tell Karl was wavering. "I like this one. I'll need the entire outfit, including accessories. Everything for the little lady, too.

Of course, we'd have to throw in some lessons. I saw that target range out back. That looks like fun.

Karl was adding up the sale in his head. This sale could be the biggest commission of the year.

Liz clicked her gum, twirled her finger around in one of her oversized hoop earrings, and winked.

The man swallowed hard, looking at her leaning against a display in her shorts and heels, and said, "I'll get that list for you. I'm sure they'll give you some tips."

The man was gone for a few minutes, returning with a short list of names and a schedule book.

He handed the list to Seth, who took it and shoved it into his pocket. "Thanks for this. It will help more than you know."

"Let's look at the practice range schedule and see what's open."

"Babe, what's a good day for you?" Seth said, keeping up the illusion and draping his arm around Liz's shoulder.

Liz leaned into Seth and whispered loudly enough for Karl to hear. "You know I have those community hours to serve for passing that bad check. I need to check in with my parole officer."

Karl backtracked fast. "Maybe we better put that scheduling off until you purchase the necessary equipment." He could see his big fat commission flying out the window. He was not about to take a bogus check from anybody.

"Aw damn. I wanted to see you shoot a bull's eye for me, Chief," Liz drawled, clicking her gum and running her fingers down her cleavage.

She watched Karl as he watched her fingers. Liz brought them up to her lips, wet the tips, and ran one over her lips. She thought Karl was going to pass out.

"Well, Karl, sorry about that, but I don't want my little darling here in jail again. I do miss her when that happens. I'll get back to you as soon as we talk to her parole officer."

Back in the truck, they could see Karl looking at them through the window. They waited until they were out of the parking lot before bursting out laughing until their sides hurt.

Catching his breath, Seth said, "That was mean."

"Yeah, it was," Liz said, bursting out laughing again.

# Chapter Twenty-One

Professor Newsom puttered in his greenhouse, a Mozart concerto playing softly in the background.

He didn't hear the student coming up behind him. "He, prof," Malcolm Fletcher said, startling the older man and making him drop the orchid he was working with. The sound cracked through the glass house like a gunshot.

"What are you doing here, Malcolm?" Newsom said, turning the music off.

"I talked with the FWC deputies. I might have headed them in your direction. I saw you in the preserve the day Hernandez was killed. There might be a bit more information I can give them."

Fletcher was looking at the orchids on the benches lining both sides of the greenhouse. He knew some of them were illegal imports.

He leaned over a pot here and there to inspect or smell the flowers. "It's like this, prof: I need at least a B in your class to graduate and get my degree. Give me what I need, and I never saw what you were up to in the preserve. I could even help you hide your little collection here before the FWC officers charge in with their warrant to search the place. I also know you are trying to propagate ghost orchids and are receiving and distributing illegal orchids. You see, I know a lot of things about a lot of people on this campus. It's kinda my business. I'm what they call a facilitator. You collect rare orchids. I might have made some connections happen."

Newsom was stunned. He walked between the benches and back, pondering what to do.

The botany professor was known among the students underground for letting overdue papers slide or bumping up a grade for a price. He was a man with few scruples.

Some people are addicted to alcohol, gambling, or drugs. He was addicted to rare orchids. The rarer, the better.

"Say I give you what you want. How do I know you will keep your end of the deal?"

"You don't," Malcolm said, walking away.

Newsom had to protect his orchids at all costs. He picked up a heavy terracotta clay pot, weighing it in his hand, and made his decision. His mind was made up. He caught up to Malcolm and swung the pot as hard as he could, hitting his target in the back of his head.

"Oh shit, what have I done?" He cursed, looking at the bleeding body at his feet. Dropping the pot, Newsom took a breath. How to get rid of the body?

After a couple seconds, it came to him. He backed up his Subaru SUV close to the body and, with great difficulty, managed to stuff Malcolm Fletcher into the back, covering him with a tarp.

He leaned against the tailgate, sweating from the exertion—his back hurt as he stumbled around and swung himself into the car.

Newsom's hands gripped the wheel so tightly they hurt as he drove along Alligator Alley towards Big Cypress Preserve.

He stopped to chat with the ranger on duty. "I'm taking some more photos on the south loop trail. There are some species of Sarraceniaceae I'm interested in."

"What the hell is that?" the ranger said.

"That's a pitcher plant. The kind that traps insects."

"Oh, like the Venus fly trap?"

"Yes, that's right. I have to go before I lose the light."

As he pulled past the ranger station, he chuckled to himself. He'd find the perfect spot and give the gators a little extra treat.

# Chapter Twenty-Two

The sun rose, casting deep purple and flamingo pink against the remaining clouds from the evening shower.

The trail was slick from the rain, with mud grabbing the tires and causing the truck to slide. Liz held on to the door handle while Seth cursed under his breath.

"It's not funny. We get stuck out here. It's either a long walk back or a long wait for someone to haul us out." Seth said, growling.

"Aw, Chief, think of it like an amusement park ride," Liz laughed.

Seth couldn't help looking over at Liz. He shook his head and smiled. "You always try to find the bright side."

"Most of the time."

They were pulling up to one of the more remote campgrounds on the North Loop Trail, which was still accessible by vehicle.

There were only two tents set up. One, a bright orange, was still zipped, indicating that whoever was inside was not stirring yet.

The other was open, and a twenty-something-year-old man in a tee shirt and shorts was trying to sort out a small propane camp grill to make some coffee.

"Let's give him a hand. Looks like he could use it," Seth said, stepping out of the truck.

Their approach startled the young man, making him drop the directions he was studying. "Shit, I didn't think anyone was around here. Sorry, I didn't hear you dive up. I can't get this darn thing to light up." He brushed his hand off his shorts and extended it to Seth. "I'm Todd Jessup. My girlfriend Helen is washing up in the little stream over there."

"I'm Officer Seth Grayson with the Florida Fish and Wildlife Commission, and this is my partner, Officer Liz Corday." Seth did not advertise that they were man and wife on the job.

Suddenly, from beyond the palmettos, scrub brush, and pines, screams echoed through the morning stillness.

"That's Helen," Todd yelled and raced toward the sound.

Seth and Liz ran with him, knowing it could be anything from an alligator to a bear.

Helen crashed full force into Todd. Out of breath, tears streaming down her face, she managed to say, "Dead body, or at least I think he's dead."

Todd held Helen. His legs and arms were scratched and bleeding from the sharp palmetto spines where he pushed through to rescue his frightened girlfriend.

Seth and Liz waited for Helen to catch her breath. When she had calmed down and was able to talk, Liz asked, "Can you take us to where you saw the body?"

Helen looked at Liz. Her eyes red-rimmed from crying, she gasped, "Do I have to?"

"It would be faster if you could."

The young woman closed her eyes and, taking a deep breath, nodded yes.

Holding tight to Todd, Helen took the path to the stream beyond the trees.

As they walked the path, Todd looked at the bloody scratches on his arms, now attracting flies, "Why didn't I think of taking the path?"

Seth clapped him on the shoulder. "We don't always think straight when someone we love is in danger." He was looking at Liz when he said it, remembering when Liz fell into the alligator pit and was almost an alligator's dinner.

Helen stopped and pointed to the body of a man lying halfway in the swift running stream beside a downed tree limb. She turned her head into Todd's chest, leaving wet spots on his shirt.

Seth leaned over the cold, wet body wedged in beside a fallen tree. The water lapping under the man's body was cold from last night's rain.

Checking for a pulse just to be sure, Seth paused listening and looked at Liz, "Damn, Liz, call for an ambulance. He's got a faint pulse, but it's there."

Liz quickly made the call.

"Oh my God," Helen breathed, dropping to her knees.

Todd knelt beside her. "You probably saved his life finding him."

Liz stood by Seth as he carefully turned the man over. She looked closer, carefully removed some wet debris from his face, and gasped.

"He's the student we met at Miami University, Malcolm Fletcher. How did he end up out here like this?"

"I don't know, but he's suffering from hypothermia and has a huge bloody cut on the side of his head. He needs to get out of this water now."

Liz enlisted Todd to help move Malcolm out of the water and sent Helen to get a blanket to warm him up.

The officers received a call stating that EMTs were en route. It would take about half an hour to reach them. The Techs told them to warm the victim slowly and do what they could for him until they arrived.

Seth also called the ranger station and Collier County Sheriff to inform them of the situation. Before long, the area would be flooded with emergency vehicles and flashing lights.

# Chapter Twenty-Three

It was stressful waiting until they heard the wail of a siren coming their way: the last to arrive and most needed to care for the victim was the ambulance.

Liz and Helen went to meet whoever was coming, leaving Todd and Seth to watch over Malcolm Fletcher.

When they reached the campsite, the owner of the other tent was up and in a rage. "What the hell is going on here? I came for some peace, and it's been nonstop all night and day."

The bellowing man wore boxer shorts and a well-worn, torn, and stained T-shirt. He sported a scraggly beard and mustache.

He looked amused when the Collier County Sheriff's unit pulled up. "Why am I not surprised," he said, rubbing his beard and crawling back into his tent.

Liz was pleased to see Sheriff Woodson and Deputy Franklin exiting one of the vehicles.

Shaking hands, Liz said, "Boy, am I glad to see you two."

"Heard you have a bit of a mystery on your hands," Sheriff Woodson said.

"Come on and meet the victim."

"I thought you had a dead body?"

"We did, too, until Seth checked his pulse. He's suffering from hypothermia and has a bad gash on his head."

When they reached the scene, Seth was talking to Malcolm,

trying to help him make sense of what had happened.

Sheriff Woodson tapped Seth on the shoulder, nodding for him to step away. "You get much out of him?"

"Naw, he's pretty far out of it. The sooner he gets to the hospital, the better."

Deputy Franklin was wandering around, "You say he was in the water. How come the alligators didn't chew him up?"

"He was only partially in the water. Fletcher was between the shore and the downed tree. The gators couldn't pull him in over that tree, so they left him alone. They're basically lazy. If whoever had dumped him had left him a few feet more in either direction, nothing might be left of him to investigate."

Janice Franklin had been with the department for ten years and asked a lot of questions. Her forehead wrinkled as she thought, "How do you know he was dropped here and not just fell over in the dark?"

"Come here, I'll show you," Seth said.

Crouching down, he pointed to tire tracks leading to where they had found Malcolm. "I'd say an SUV."

"Why an SUV?" Franklin asked.

"It's the width between the tires, for one thing. Besides, Malcolm Fletcher was a tall person, six feet or thereabout. Could you see anyone folding him into the trunk of a sedan?"

"He's right, Franklin. Officer Grayson is one of the smartest people I know who to survey a crime scene," Sheriff Woodson said. "Take a cast of that tire tread and hand it over to the crime scene boys. See what they can do with it,"

The ambulance arrived at the campsite, and Liz showed the technicians how to access the victim. As Fletcher was carried past on the stretcher, he grabbed Liz by the sleeve and whispered, "Newsom."

"I've had enough and want to go home," Helen said, sitting on a camp chair, her face in her hands.

"Yes, you can go home, but leave your contact information with Sheriff Woodson and us. You and Todd will have to fill out statements," Liz said.

Todd put his arms around Helen, "I'm so sorry. This has not been much of a vacation for you."

"Next time I pick the place, it definitely will not include alligators, mosquitoes, tents without air conditioning, and finding an almost dead body."

"You got a deal."

# Chapter Twenty-Four

The indignant bearded man was busy throwing his camping gear in the back of an old pickup truck.

Sheriff Woodson walked over and stood in front of him. "Whoa, we need some information before you take off."

"Last I checked, it was a free country, and I don't see any shackles. I want outa here and not dragged into somethin' that ain't none a my business."

The Sheriff persisted. "I need to see an ID."

"Oh no, you don't." The man stood defiantly with his hand on his hips.

"In the State of Florida, it is a first-degree misdemeanor if you do not produce identification when asked by a police officer. So yes, you do."

That took the wind out of the man's sails. He dug around in the back pocket of his grubby jeans and produced a tattered wallet. Opening the wallet, he thumbed through it until he pulled out an equally grubby driver's license.

Looking everywhere but at the Sheriff, he handed the license over.

Straining to see the expiration date, Woodson said. "You have got to be kidding me. This license expired in 2008."

"I don't drive much." The man cringed.

"By any chance, is that truck registered and insured?"

The man, who still had not provided his name, looked up to the sky and pursed his lips. "I don't believe it is. I'd never lie to an officer of the law."

Sheriff Woodson hung his head in disbelief. "Can you at least give me your name and address?" wondering if it would match the license.

"My name is Max Weller, of no fixed abode." The man said, rather pleased with himself.

"Franklin, get over here. Please run our friend here, Max Weller, through the system and see what comes up."

"Mr. Weller, is there anything in your tent, truck, or on your person that I should be aware of? Is there anything that could poke, stick, or otherwise injure me?"

"Not so long as you're careful."

The Sheriff asked, "What is that supposed to mean?"

"I been camping. I got knives in my gear. There're plenty sharp. I have to eat off the land as much as possible. I don't have a steady income, if you know what I mean."

Weller ducked into his day-glow orange tent, digging around his scruffy belongings, and produced a couple knives. One of which was a very lethal-looking hunting knife.

Sheriff Woodson knew that a good hunting knife was not cheap. He turned it over a bit before asking. "How did you afford something like this?"

"Well, I kinda found it."

"What do you mean you kinda found it?"

"It was in this guy's truck, and he wasn't gonna be comin' back for it."

"What the hell does that mean?" the sheriff was getting impatient with Weller not getting to the point.

Weller looked down at his grimy bare feet and drew circles in the sandy dirt with his toes. "Well, ya see. This truck was parked by one of the oil rigs.

" The guy in the truck is watching an old guy wearing a back-pack try to reach for one of the white orchids in the cypress trees.

" All of a sudden, this arrow comes flying through the air and sticks in the tree right above the old guy's head.

" I thought it was the guy from the truck, but the guy from the truck was as confused as the old man. They both look around but can't see anyone.

"The truck guy walks up to the orchid guy and starts yelling at him about how the orchids were protected, and the older guy had no business trying to take 'em. I heard the truck guy say he was there to protect the Florida Panthers, and that he was from the Florida Wildlife Federation and had trail cameras set up and would report the orchid man to the authorities."

Sheriff Woodson stops him there, "We didn't get any reports about anyone taking ghost orchids from the preserve."

"The truck guy didn't get the chance. That's what I'm trying to tell you. When he turned to leave, the orchid guy clocked him with a big rock. The old man was stronger than I thought."

"How come they didn't see you?"

"I was on the other side of this stream and hidden by a stand of palmettos. I was collecting palmetto berries. I get so much a pound for them, and boy, do I need the money."

"You do know that collecting palmetto berries is against the law."

"Ain't everything?"

"Aren't you worried about going to jail? Harvesting saw palmetto berries without a permit gets you up to five years in prison."

"I get paid about seven dollars a pound for the darn things an figure it's worth the risk. A guy's got to eat, ya know."

Things were starting to fall into place, but that still didn't solve the problem of who shot the arrow and where the trail cameras had gone.

Deputy Franklin stood uneasy beside the Sheriff, trying to get his attention. "I have information on Mr. Weller."

"You going to keep it to yourself or tell me?" Exasperated, the Sheriff had had enough and wanted to clear up this nonsense fast.

"Mr. Weller has several outstanding warrants, mostly for

vagrancy, driving without a license, driving without insurance, and an unregistered vehicle. He has missed multiple court appearances and has outstanding fines and warrants."

"Mr. Weller, we are going to put you under arrest. Please put your hands behind your back. We will add the harvesting of saw palmetto berries without a permit to the list."

Max Weller cooperated. He didn't need resisting arrest to be added to his list of crimes. Besides, he could get a hot shower and decent food in jail.

Woodson called Officer Grayson on his way and told Seth what he had found out. Seth wanted to talk to Weller more about the missing trail cameras. This could explain who killed Adam Hernandez and why, but that still didn't explain who shot the arrow into the tree above the professor's head. Another question was, who tried to kill Malcolm Fletcher? That person was still out there.

# Chapter Twenty-Five

Seth and Liz followed the ambulance to the hospital. The closest emergency center was in Naples.

The trip seemed to take forever. The officers needed to speak to Fletcher as soon as he was able to talk.

"I wonder what Malcolm meant when he said Newsom? Did he want us to contact the professor and inform him that Malcolm was hurt or that Newsom caused his injury?" Liz said.

"We'll have to wait and ask Malcolm when we talk to him." Seth had to spend precious time searching for a parking space. Finally, he found one several rows away from the emergency entrance. "I hate hospitals. The parking system never makes sense to me. A family in a crisis should not have to cruise a parking lot for fifteen minutes."

"Calm down, Chief. Let's go and see what's happening with Malcolm." Liz was starting to get a feeling that something was bothering Seth, but she couldn't put her finger on it.

Liz took over and introduced themselves to the receptionist, showing their badges and asking about Malcolm Fletcher.

The receptionist directed them to a small room down the hall. Nurses and technicians hustled in and out of the room past them.

Seth and Liz tried not to get in the way and stood against the wall opposite the door.

They could see Malcolm with lines running into his arms and

monitors beeping. A young doctor stood beside the bed, flashing a light in the young man's eyes.

The doctor issued orders to one of the nurses and left the room.

"Excuse me, doctor. We're officers with the Florida Wildlife Commission and found Mr. Fletcher. Can you tell us his condition and when we can speak with him? We'd like to know what happened to him." Seth said.

"I can't tell you much. Mr. Fletcher is in bad shape. He has a concussion and is suffering from hypothermia. I've ordered an MRI to assess the extent of the damage. I'll know more after that."

"When will he be able to talk to us?"

"He's semi-conscious now but not making much sense. I'd say after the MRI, and he warms up. Give him a couple hours."

Liz put her hand on Seth's sleeve, "Thanks, doctor, we'll be back later."

The heat bounced off the tarmac as they returned to their parking spot. Opening the truck door was like opening the door to an oven.

Seth reached in, turned on the engine, and set the air conditioning to high. They waited for the truck to cool down a bit before getting in.

Seth's phone rang loudly in his pocket. "Hey, what's up?"

Liz could only watch the one-sided conversation as Seth answered in single syllables.

Liz waited for him to hang up. "OK, who was that, and what did they say?" Liz asked, annoyed and curious.

Seth removed his hat to wipe the sweat dripping in his eyes. His hair, black as a raven's wing, stirred in the heated breeze as he looked smugly at Liz, "That, sweetheart, was my competition, Agent Miller. We have the warrant to search Professor Newsom's house, grounds, and car."

Liz came around the car and snuggled up to Seth, "He's not any competition to you, my darling," she said, nibbling on his ear. "There is only one man for me, and that's you." She hoped that's what was bothering her husband. The agent had made a pass at her when they first met and always seemed to get Seth riled up whenever he was around.

"Is having Pat around again what's got your war paint on?' Liz said, getting in the passenger side of the truck.

"That and this case," Seth said. "OK, I'm jealous. He has a fancy Federal job, working out of D.C.. He flies all over the states to all the National Parks. I see the way he looks at you. I like the guy, but you know…" Seth shrugged.

Liz turned in her seat to face Seth. "Did you ever think he might be jealous of you? You have a great job, and we make a great team on and off that job. We live near your very supportive parents and family. I know our captains and the other law enforcement agencies we work with know and trust us."

Liz put her head down and came back with a silly smile. "Just because he's tall and incredibly handsome does not mean you have any reason to be jealous of him."

Liz slid over the center console and onto Seth's lap, kissing him passionately. His body responded, "Oh Christ, Liz." He didn't want to let her go. He looked deep into her eyes and shook his head.

"God, you drive me crazy. We're in a public parking lot," Seth said, pushing her gently away and looking around. "Wait until we get home." He smiled and kissed her back quickly.

"Oh, spoiled sport." Liz pretended to sulk, sliding back to the passenger side of the truck.

The AC had done its job, and they both needed to cool down. Seth put the truck in gear and took off to meet Agent Miller at Professor Newsom's home.

# Chapter Twenty-Six

Pat was waiting for them when they arrived. Newsom's one-story Florida ranch home was a thirty-minute drive from the University, where prices were slightly lower. His Subaru was in the drive. Even on a professor's salary, Coral Gables would be a stretch.

"I wonder how he affords this place?" Liz asked as they parked.

"Hey, you guys ready for this? I saw Newsom peeking out the window as I drove up."

"Yeah. Let's do it." Seth said. Not knowing what to expect, he undid the snap on his holster. Liz and Pat did the same.

Pat knocked and rang the doorbell, "Professor Newsom, I'm a Federal Wildlife Officer with a warrant to search your property. Please open the door."

Behind them, the Collier County Sheriff's deputies arrived to help with the search.

Newsom opened the door slowly. "What is this all about?"

"We have reason to believe you have been collecting protected orchid species from the Big Cypress National Park."

"That's outrageous. I would never do such a thing." The professor's face was turning red with anger.

Pat signaled the deputies to proceed, handed the warrant to Newsom, and pushed past the fuming professor.

Liz and Seth decided to take the outbuildings, beginning with the greenhouse.

The greenhouse was climate-controlled, setting the perfect temperature and humidity for the rare orchids. Walking down the center aisle, the deputies didn't see any ghost orchids.

"I don't know about you, but we need someone who knows about orchids here. I can't tell one from the other." Liz said.

Seth looked over the benches of orchids, "Is it me, or are there a lot of empty spaces?" He ran his hand over one of the spaces, and his fingers came away with fresh dirt. "Something has been recently moved from here."

"The professor was in a hurry to hide something he didn't want anyone to find."

"I think you're right. I want to show you something I spotted outside."

Turning to follow, Liz tripped over something half-hidden under one of the benches.

Catching herself, she pulled out a green backpack and tossed it on the bench. "What do we have here?"

Seth helped her open the pack. Surprise showed on both their faces. "Now we know where the missing trail cameras went."

"I wonder why he took all the cameras? Unless they caught him stealing the orchids?" Liz said, shrugging her shoulders.

"Or worse." Seth looked at Liz, and she caught his meaning. Could Professor Newsom have killed Adam Hernandez?

"Let me show you what I saw outside."

Seth carried the heavy backpack out of the greenhouse and dropped it beside some tire tracks in the gravel.

"Wait, where is Newsom's car?" Seth said, looking around. He quickly dialed Agent Miller.

"Pat, Newsom took off. Did anyone see him go?"

"Shit, the sheriff's outfit was supposed to keep an eye on him."

"Well, they didn't." Seth was upset that Newsom got away.

Hanging up, he turned his attention back to Liz. "There are some tire tracks out here that match the ones that were by the stream where Malcolm Fletcher's body was dumped, and see here, a broken flower pot with blood on it."

Liz looked at the tracks and the pot. "He seemed like such a sweet old man, just a frumpy old college professor. Guess you never know what's happening inside someone's head when they're desperate enough."

Agent Miller joined them, "We're about finished with the house. There is nothing unusual there, just a lot of books everywhere. What have you found.?"

"These tracks match the ones we found where Malcolm Fletcher was dumped, and there is blood on this broken piece of flowerpot," Seth said, handing Pat the blood-stained piece of pottery so the agent could save it for evidence. It was dropped into an evidence bag and sealed.

"I'll call the boys over to take a cast of the track to match the tread on the professor's car and at the scene where you found Fletcher. We didn't find any evidence of orchids in the house."

"There is evidence of plants being recently removed from the greenhouse. We need an orchid expert here to tell us if any of the remaining orchids are illegal to possess," Seth said.

"Question, if he did take ghost orchids from the preserve, what did he do with them?"

Deputy Franklin came running up from the house, waving a piece of paper in her hands. She stopped in front of the Sheriff and handed him the paper.

"It's a receipt for a storage unit, a climate-controlled storage unit." Sheriff Woodson said, staring at the receipt through a plastic evidence bag.

"Want to make a bet where the ghost orchids are?" Agent Miller said.

"We need to get to this warehouse before Newsom can move any illegal orchids or, worse, destroy them.

# Chapter Twenty-Seven

The warehouse was a few miles from the university. Newsom's car was parked in front of an old industrial building that had been converted into storage units. A large, new-looking green transit van with New York plates was beside it, with the back doors open. Pat, Sheriff Woodson, and Deputy Franklin pulled up at the same time as Seth and Liz.

Sheriff Woodson held back. Talking over the radio to Agent Miller, he asked, " Hold on a minute. I have to check that I'm in Collier County. I could get my ass handed to me on a plate if I get this wrong." Woodson called up the address on his patrol vehicle computer and breathed a sigh of relief. "It's OK, agent. We are just inside the county line in Collier County. My boys and I are ready when you are."

They got out and closed their doors softly, not to alert Newsom and whoever was inside with him.

They approached cautiously, weapons drawn, ready for anything. Loud voices came from inside the warehouse.

"Our clients are not patient people. They pay for a service and expect a product to arrive as promised. These connections are very wealthy and have, shall we say, connections that make breaking a promise unacceptable."

The warehouse door was open, only a crack. Liz could see a man dressed in black facing Newsom. He was gray-haired, about fifty, and carried himself with an air of authority.

Two other men stood behind him equipped with shoulder holsters, and she was sure another gun was tucked behind their shirts in the back. The men were taller and had the build of those used to weapons and following orders.

Beyond Newsom and the men were two rows of benches with orchids. Liz spotted a couple that she was sure were ghost orchids. The orchid expert would have to confirm the rest.

She stepped away from the door and relayed what she saw.

"Go in quiet and find some cover. We have to hear what these guys are up to," Pat said.

The team gently opened the door and stealthily moved around, keeping close to the walls and finding cover behind shipping crates and packing material.

"Look, Mr. Bandaleri. I can only send what the importers bring me. You must realize it's a risky trade for them." Newsom said, his voice quivering with fear. "I don't know what is in the other packages, and I don't want to know."

"Oh, I do know there is a risk. That's why my clients are willing to pay a premium for their merchandise," the man Bandaleri said with a heavy New York accent. "Now, I want you to pack up all the ghost orchids you have. I have buyers waiting for them. I will be collecting the other packages as well."

"But I'm trying to propagate the ghost orchids so I don't have to collect them from the preserve. I can't go back there to get more."

"That's your problem."

Newsom grabbed one of the ghost orchids and held it firmly in place. "At least let me keep one. If I can learn how to propagate it, you will have more than you need at a cheaper price."

"Sounds reasonable, but no." the arrogant man nodded to his men, and one of them ripped the orchid from Newsom's hands. The other whipped a gun out and pointed it at Newsom.

"I will take the ghost and your other rare orchids as well. Call it the price of doing business. You are but a middleman. I'm thinking of taking my business elsewhere. The orchids are only part of my business."

Shouting to one of his men, "You, start loading up the van." One of the heavies grabbed a couple of the orchid pots and followed out to the van.

The loud click of a bullet entering its chamber filled the warehouse as the remaining thug smiled. Showing a nicely capped gold incisor.

Newsom stood there, shock and bewilderment etched on his face, a gun pointed at his chest—a wet stain spreading across his crotch.

# Chapter Twenty-Eight

Newsom stood shaking with his eyes closed. When nothing happened, he dared to open one eye.

He could not believe his luck and collapsed in a heap on the floor when he saw Agent Miller standing behind the gunman with a gun firmly pressed against the man's neck. Seth was there to relieve the gunman of his weapon.

"You can get up now," Seth said to the quivering man on the floor.

Newsom was speechless. He had almost died, yet he also knew that consequences were coming.

Pat cuffed the gunman and marched him outside.

Seth helped Newsom stand, cuffed the professor, and led him out to join the others.

Bandaleri had walked right into Liz's waiting arms and was now in a patrol car with Deputy Franklin guarding him. The other two were cuffed and awaiting transport, which was coming around the corner. They will go to the county lockup for holding for now.

Newsom would go with Agent Miller. He had a lot to answer for—trading in the illegal importation of endangered orchids and the murder of a federal agent.

Liz wanted to question him about the ghost orchids. The Florida Fish and Wildlife Commission oversees the illegal importation of plants and animals in accordance with the CITES agreement.

She didn't want to let that go. Jurisdiction can become quite complex, with multiple agencies vying for a piece of the action.

Pat was very interested in seeing what was on the trail camera that the professor had stolen from the preserve. He planned on getting everyone together to view what the cameras had recorded. They might even show an image of who was shooting the arrows.

"Sheriff, can we use your station to see what might be on the trail cameras?" Pat said.

"Sure, I'm interested too. We get to fight over jurisdiction. Newsom allegedly killed your federal agent, Adam Hernandez, in the preserve and stole the cameras. I guess you get to share the trafficking of the rare orchids with the FWC," Woodson rocked back on his heels, "but I get the attempted murder of Malcolm Fletcher. That sound good to you?"

"Sounds good to me. I'll meet you back there."

The cavalcade of law enforcement vehicles pulled out and headed for Naples and the Collier County sheriff's headquarters.

Before entering the station, Pat made a call to D.C. about Bandaleri and what he had overheard. There might be more than illegal orchids at play here, he told them. He was surprised to find out that Bandaleri was already on their radar in connection with one of the Columbian cartels.

When the agent hung up, he wondered what his friends had gotten themselves into this time.

# Chapter Twenty-Nine

Newsom was deposited in an interview room and would answer questions later, along with Bandaleri.

Shutting down Bandaleri's illegal import of rare and endangered orchids was a major coup for the FWC deputies.

The sheriff's staff set up one of the conference rooms to view the footage from the trail cameras on a large-screen TV.

Coffee and donuts were provided while the connections were made to the TV, and everyone found a seat. It was standing room only for some of the deputies.

The first few minutes were fairly dull until a panther, and its cub passed in front of one of the cameras.

"Oh, Seth, look, a real panther and her cub," Liz said. " I wish I could see one in the park someday."

Seth reached out to take her hand and squeeze it. "Maybe someday you will, Sweetheart."

Moving on to another camera, they all stopped talking to watch Professor Newsom pass in front of one of the cameras.

The next camera picked him up, walking up to the tree with the ghost orchid. He dropped his backpack and reached for the orchid when Adam Hernandez entered the frame. They exchange heated words when an arrow flies out of nowhere and lands in the tree near the ghost orchid. Both men are shocked and look around to see who shot the arrow.

After a few more intense words, Hernandez turns to leave. The professor picks up a large stone and hits the other man over the head, knocking him to the ground.

"That proves he killed Agent Hernandez," Deputy Franklin shouts.

"Not so fast, wait." Agent Miller said.

They watched as the professor gathered the ghost orchids from the tree and carefully placed them in a container in his backpack. He looks at Hernandez on the ground and shakes his head, turning to run, but something stops him. He appears to be listening to something or someone.

Newsom hesitates and sees Hernandez struggling to get up. Panic is written on his face.

The deputies and officers see Newsom approach the trail camera, and the camera goes dark.

The lights come up, and everyone breathes again.

Agent Miller steps to the front. "We can see that the professor hit Agent Hernandez and knocked him unconscious. We have two questions. Who fired the arrow, and who or what was Newsom listening to that spooked him?

"Another question: did that person finish what Newsom started and kill Hernandez? We have to find everyone who was in the park that day. Sheriff, your deputies can help with that. Ask all the park rangers to review their visitor logbooks. I'll work with Seth and Liz and check out the campgrounds for long-term campers."

Sheriff Woodson took over. "I want everyone on this first thing tomorrow morning. I want results."

They split the park between the Collier County Sheriff's Department and the National Park Service Rangers to check the visitors and day campers at Burns Lake, Monroe Lake, and along Loop Road and Eleven Mile Road. That would cover most of the Tamiami Trail that intersected the Park.

Seth, Liz, and Agent Miller would take off-road vehicles and start with the more remote sections of the park, focusing on the long-term campers and hunters.

Pat also had a surprise in store, placing a large black case on the table. He brought out a fancy drone. "This thing will help get a bird's eye view of the park."

# Chapter Thirty

Unloading their vehicles at the Main Welcome Center, they stopped to plan their routes.

"I'd like to take the Bear Island Unit of the park. There are several camping areas up that way," Pat said.

"Liz and I will take the Corn Dance Unit. That's where Professor Newsom had his run-in with Agent Hernandez." Seth said

"The oil company has a processing plant at Raccoon Point in that unit. I've been reading up on that. It's pretty controversial what they are doing." Liz said.

Seth shook his head, "That's my genius. Always reading up on things. If you ever want to know something, ask Liz." Seth hugged his wife and kissed her on the cheek.

Revving up the OTVs, they took off.

Agent Miller traveled north on Turner River Road. He stopped halfway and unpacked the state-of-the-art drone.

Sending it skyward, he scouted west over Deep Lake Unit. There was no camping in that unit, but it didn't hurt to check it out. He did the same with the Turner Lake Unit. That was a large section of the preserve with no long-term camping but lots of off-trail vehicle (OTV) trails for hunters. It would take one person days to cover it all. The drone did all the work.

The drone captured images of other off-road vehicles (OTVs) in the park, hikers, and wildlife.

His drone had a built-in camera, and he took some pictures of the wildlife. He couldn't wait to show Liz the image of another panther and her cubs.

Bringing the drone down, he carried it onto the campgrounds.

There were three checkpoints, and he inquired at each one about the visitors and whether they all appeared to be routine park visitors and campers. All the checkpoints reported nothing out of the ordinary.

Pat checked out the campsites, introduced himself, and wished everyone a safe stay in the park.

He hoped that Seth and Liz were coming up with something. At least he had some nice images and got to play with a cool toy for the afternoon.

# Chapter Thirty-One

S eth and Liz drove on an improved road for most of the way until it ended, and the OTV trails began. The trails were like a spiderweb winding off into the distant areas of the park.

They bounced along the rutted trail left by the massive tires of the drilling equipment before coming to the crime scene.

In the distance, a drill head shimmered in the afternoon heat, like an ancient beast dipping its head to drink from the earth, rising to dip over and over again. The processing plant was located further on at Raccoon Point.

"Let's look around by the drill rig," Seth said. "I have a feeling everything started there."

Circling the rig, Seth wanted a closer look and shut down the OTV. The rig had been in operation for decades. The Florida weather had done its worst.

The ground around one of the pipes was stained with a dark, sludgy substance. The rusting pipe showed signs of a new fitting. "Someone has fixed a leak here recently," Seth said. Taking a smear of the spilled oil between his fingers, Seth looked at the thick, viscous substance. "This is not the crude oil they refine for gasoline. This stuff is only good for greasing motor parts and things like that. It can't be worth much. It's not worth the damage it's doing to the ecosystem here."

Seth walked around the area, stepping carefully and using the skills he had learned from his father while living on the reservation. "I can see the signs of the work boots that did the repair, but under that are signs of a struggle. Look closely. You can just about make it out," Seth pointed in the dirt, "You can see a set of work boots facing hiking boots like those Hernandez wore. Maybe a push and shove between the two men. The one facing Adam had a star-shaped design on his boot heel. That's pretty distinctive."

Liz crouched down beside Seth and looked closely. "You're right, Chief. I can just make it out. You think Hernandez confronted someone here about the leak?"

Seth stood staring at the ground for several seconds. Liz could feel his mind sensing what happened to Hernandez.

"Remember in the video from the trail camera, Newsom looks this way, like he sees someone?"

"Yeah, it shook him up."

"Yeah, I do. I also think that person is the one that killed Hernandez."

"Let's see if anyone is home at the processing plant."

The plant looked all but deserted. Rust stains dripped off the sides of the massive storage tanks. Large and small pipes carrying the crude oil to be processed ran between the tanks. Signs of tanker truck tires rutted the roads.

Liz was upset at the environmental destruction the trucks caused by passing back and forth to the refinery.

Off to one side was an OTV capable of taking several passengers. A small office structure was the only building.

The officers parked beside the OTV and listened to hear any sounds of voices in the office. A radio played 70s music inside.

"Maybe someone is home after all," Liz said.

"Let's hope they don't mind unexpected company," Seth said, stepping off the OTV. He walked over to the other OTV and looked at the boot prints in the sandy ground as he circled the vehicle.

"Our man was here. At least his boots were."

"Let's pay him a visit," Liz said.

"We can't go in guns a blazing. We need proof, and a name

would be a good start."

The radio cut off when they knocked on the door. A tall man with a scruffy beard wearing a short-sleeved shirt and jeans jerked open the door, shouting, "You lost?"

Liz jumped back, startled.

Standing his ground, Seth said, "No, we are Florida Fish and Wildlife Commission Deputies. I thought we'd check in and ask about a recent leak that was detected."

"That was fixed," the man said and was about to close the door.

"We need to file a report, including the time, date, and the name of the person who made the repair to make it official. Who did you report it to? What is the name of the person reporting it? It's an environmental concern in the park." Seth was working his way inside the office.

Liz followed with her hand on her holster. She didn't trust the man. There was just something volatile about him, like playing with dynamite and matches.

The radio in the office crackled, "Sully, what the hell are you playing at? I need the read-out for that pressure valve."

Sully, startled, picked up the handheld radio, "Yeah, boss, but we got company. Two nosey FWC officers."

"Shit, I'm on my way."

The big man scratched his beard, "You guys got a form or something we got to fill out?"

"We didn't think anyone would be here," Seth said. "Just thought we would look around for anything else that might need to be reported."

"Hump." The man, Sully, snorted.

Liz wandered around the stuffy office, looking at the maps on the wall. One of them showed the locations of the drill pads. She counted about ten active wells. Liz loved research and would look up more information when they got home later.

The office door flew open and banged against the wall. A man of average height but well-muscled stood shadowed in the doorway. Stepping into the room, the light from the single window revealed a weathered face and a nose that had seen more than one fight. He carried himself with an air that demanded respect and got it. He wore an expression of pure meanness.

Sully handed him the pressure readout, squeezed his bulk past the man, and exited as quickly as possible.

"OK, I'm the project manager, Nick Halleran. You got issues. You talk to me."

Seth knew the man was trying to intimidate him, but it didn't work.

"As your man Sully said, my partner and I are with the Florida Fish and Wildlife Commission about a leak. It was not reported. We saw that it was fixed, which is great, but it should have been reported." Seth stood his ground.

"What's the big deal? It's fixed."

"I'm sure you know how an oil leak harms the environment," Liz said. "We need to know how long it was leaking before it was fixed. An oil leak can spread to the aquifer and poison the water for several miles." Liz was furious that the man didn't seem to care about the impact the leak might cause.

"I don't know how long it was leaking. We fixed it as soon as one of our men found it. This other guy was snooping around and asking questions. He had a badge; he claimed to be from a federal agency and wanted the leak fixed. I sent Sully out to fix it, which should have been the end of it. Now you all turn up. This is harassment. I've got a business to run. Now get the hell out of my office and take it up with corporate." Halleran turned and stormed out of the office, not bothering to close the door.

Liz said with her hand on her hips, "Now that went well."

"I think Sully is the one that killed Adam Hernandez. Proving it is the problem."

# Chapter Thirty-Two

Leaving the processing plant, Seth stopped the OTV by a small creek. The only sound was the squeaking drone of the nearby drill head and the buzzing of cicadas in the trees.

Taking out his cell phone, Seth called Agent Miller and shared his suspicions about the man, Sully, at the processing plant and his encounter with the plant manager, Nick Halleran.

"Thanks, Seth. I'll get them both in for a word. I haven't turned up anything. I managed to capture some great shots with the drone. How about looking at them together? We might spot our arrow guy."

"Sounds like a plan. Liz and I will pick up something and meet you at our place later."

Seth had been pacing around as he talked. Liz was sitting on the OTV waiting.

Liz noticed that Seth suddenly stopped and stared across the creek. He put his finger to his lips, motioned her to be quiet, and come to him slowly.

She was terrified that he had spotted a bear. It was not uncommon for black bears to be spotted in the park. Even the occasional python was found.

He turned her to face the creek and whispered, "Look at the base of the cypress between the palmettos."

Liz could not believe what she was seeing. A female Florida panther and her cub were watching them.

"That's got to be their prints we saw," she whispered.

"Adam Hernandez was probably tracking her and the cub when he was killed. I'll have to find out who he reported to and get someone out here."

They waited several minutes until the panther rose, turned, and vanished into the thick tangle of cypress, slash pine, and palmetto.

"I'll never forget that until the day I die," Liz said, still whispering.

"Unfortunately, if something is not done to help the panthers, our children will never see a panther in the wild," Seth said solemnly.

"Seth, look." Liz pointed high in the cypress tree above where the panther had been. A cluster of ghost orchid blooms glowed brilliant white in the rays of the afternoon sun.

Liz put her hand on Seth's arm. "Something else just crossed my mind. We need to get the water around here tested. There's no telling if that leak contaminated the streams or how far it's reached."

"I'll mention that to Pat tonight."

# Chapter Thirty-Three

Sitting at the kitchen table, Seth, Liz, and Pat discussed what they had learned so far.

Liz kept track on a notepad. "Professor Newsom tried to kill Malcolm Fletcher and feed him to the alligators because he was blackmailing the professor."

'Right, and we believe Adam Hernandez was killed over the oil leak. I'll have Nick Halleran and his man brought in tomorrow for questioning." Pat said. "I also have to call and get a replacement for Hernandez—his work on the panthers is essential, as well as get the water tested.

"The only thing we don't know is who is shooting arrows in the park. There have been three more reports of someone shooting arrows near people in the last two weeks. One was near a woman trying to pick a ghost orchid. Another was a family taking a closed trail while hiking. The last was two days ago when a man was getting ready to hunt a deer out of season. That one was a close call. The arrow landed at the man's feet. He wasn't going to report it, but his friend was so scared that the friend called it in." Seth sat back in his chair, thinking about the bow he saw in his cousin's truck.

Liz busied herself clearing up the supper dishes while Pat and Seth set up the pictures from the drone and cast them to the TV.

When it was ready, Pat set the pictures playing across the screen. The images of the park were fabulous. Liz wooed and awed over and over again.

"Wait, stop, go back. Can you bring that in closer?" Seth said, his eyes wide with anticipation as he moved to the edge of his seat. "There in that little clearing. There's a man with a crossbow. I swear it is. He's wearing camo, but he's there."

All three strained to see the man. "Yes, you're right," Pat said "There is someone there. We need to get the drone up again. He's on foot. I don't see a vehicle nearby. We can't use the OTVs. He'd hear us coming. How are you on horseback?"

Liz looked at them. Panic was written on her face. "You have got to be kidding me. The closest I got to a horse was the merry-go-round at the fair."

"Pat, you and I can borrow a couple horses from the reservation. Liz, you can operate the drone and guide us."

"You're going to have to teach me."

"Come on outside. It's like playing a video game."

Pat took Liz outside while Seth sat and watched the image on the TV screen, trying to see who the mysterious person hiking through the preserve might be. There was nothing to compare the person's height to, and he never faced the camera.

Seth could make out the crossbow, and the person was wearing camo, but that was all. Most hunters wore camo but wore an orange hat or vest to alert other hunters. This one did not.

Liz came in giggling, "That was so much fun. We have to get one of these."

"You have any luck?" Pat said, nodding at the TV.

"No. I'll call my father and have him arrange for some horses for tomorrow."

Seth picked up his phone and walked out to the back porch. Nickosi was at his heels, sensing his agitation.

Scratching the dog's head, he kept turning things over in his head. Was he missing something?

At the same time, Seth prayed that he would not have to track down one of his family members.

Seth's father asked several questions and even volunteered to ride with them. Andres offered to gather men to ride with Pat and Seth when that failed. Finally, Andres agreed to two horses and a trailer for tomorrow.

The older man was sorry he would miss out on being part of such a search in the preserve.

# Chapter Thirty-Four

Seth's father met them at the stables on the Seminole reservation just after sunrise. The two horses were saddled and ready to go. A two-horse trailer was waiting nearby, and a stable boy was there to help load the horses when they were prepared to leave.

"I've got a couple good steady horses for you," Andres said.

"Thanks, Dad. You met Special Agent Pat Miller at my house before."

"Ah yes, you had all the women giggling that day. I'll have some more python or alligator waiting for you when you get back," Andres said with a smile dancing across his usually stoic face.

Pat grimaced. "I can do without snake, but I kinda like gator."

He stood by a buckskin mare stroking her nose. "I like this one. Does she have a name?"

"We call her Lakni Tayki, Yellow Woman. She will answer to Lakni."

The agent practiced saying the name. "What about the blue roan there? What's his name?"

"His name is Looci Ooki, Blue Water. A young girl named him, and he will answer to Looci. Both are good, dependable trail horses. I can have some men ride with you and help if you want."

"I appreciate the offer, but we better do this alone."

Andres helped Seth and Pat hitch the horse trailer to Seth's truck and load the horses.

They were to meet Liz at one of the check stations along SR-41 and work through the preserve from south to north.

The person shooting the arrows seemed most active in the Corn Dance Unit, so they would look there first.

Liz would operate the drone and drive an OTV, and Pat and Seth would set out on horseback.

"You think this guy is some sort of eco-warrior trying to save the preserve?" Pat said as they made their way to the highway.

"He sees it that way." Seth was staring out the window, turning things over in his mind. Who had he seen with a crossbow? He prayed to the Breath Giver of the Seminoles that it was not his cousin. Zackery.

Zackery had invited him to meetings to protest the oil drilling in the park and the proposed change to make a large section a wilderness area, which would exclude the Seminoles and Miccosukee from using it as they had for hunting and their ceremonies. Seth regretted not going and listening to what his people had to say. He had to be more involved in his tribes' issues.

"Hey, earth to Seth," Pat said, shoving Seth to get his attention.

"Yeah, sorry, I've got my mind on this guy we're after. Sooner or later, he's going to take it too far and hit someone, maybe kill someone. We have to get him before he does."

# Chapter Thirty-Five

Liz was waiting at the checkpoint when they pulled in with the horse trailer.

"About time. There's been another attack. A kid was playing with some newly hatched turtles, and an arrow barely missed him. The parents are going crazy and have called the Sheriff."

"Where did this happen?" Seth said, stepping out of the truck.

Pat was getting ready to let the horses out of the trailer.

"Near the Monument Lake campground. The Sheriff is on his way, and he's not happy."

Seth told Pat to hold off unloading the horses, "Change of plans. We're going to the Monument Lake campgrounds. There's been a sighting, and we might be able to pick up his trail from there."

Liz jumped back on the OTV and took off, engine roaring down the road.

Pat and Seth followed after her and saw the Sheriff's patrol car in their rearview mirror coming up fast. The Sheriff sped past them and would arrive at the scene before they did.

Pat chuckled, "I hope he doesn't stop to give Liz a ticket for driving the OTV on the roadway."

"He'll get an earful if he does," Seth smiled at the thought.

Up ahead, a small crowd had gathered. Sheriff Woodson and Deputy Franklin pulled in and hurriedly tried calming the young child's parents.

Liz waited off to one side while Seth and Pat parked.

Deputy Franklin came over, nodding over her shoulder at the noise behind her. "Those people are nuts. If they catch the person that shot the arrow before you all do, I'm afraid they'll try and lynch him."

"Can you take us to where the child was playing? We might be able to pick up his trail from there. Liz has a drone, so we can also search from the air." Seth said.

"I'll get someone to take us there. You get unloaded. I'll be right back."

Deputy Franklin hurried off while the horses were offloaded and the saddles were checked.

Liz had never seen Seth on a horse before, "You look impressive up there, Chief."

"I could teach you to ride. We could do some trail riding together. It might be fun."

Liz bit her lip and approached the horse hesitantly that Seth was sitting on. She reached out and stroked the big blue roan's neck.

"He's warm and soft. I don't know what I expected."

Seth looked down at her, "You never petted a horse before?"

"I never saw one up close before. When my dad and I went camping, it was for hunting or fishing, not horseback riding. My mom would have gone nuts if she thought I was riding a horse. It was bad enough that I came home smelling of fish, all dirty and gamey."

Seth had a picture of Liz covered in mud and stinking to the high heavens, knowing her mother wanted her in pink dresses and lace.

"We'll talk to my father when we get home. There are trails on the rez we can use."

Deputy Franklin was back with a young boy. "This is Johnathan. He was with his brother when the arrow came flying. He can take you."

"Hi, Johnathan. Won't your parents miss you?" Seth said. He didn't want to get the boy in trouble or cause more problems than there were already.

"Naw, they're too busy yelling at the Sheriff to notice. Sides, it's not that far."

"Hop on with Officer Corday and lead the way."

The group took off, leaving the angry crowd behind. The Sheriff tried his best to assure the parents that all was being done to catch the culprit who shot the arrow and that they could resume their camping trip.

Johnathan led them a short distance away to a trickling stream. Palmettos and water oaks lined the banks, their branches entwined with trailing Spanish moss that dripped moisture from the humid air. A small beach led to moss-covered rocks and a large branch where a couple adult turtles basked in the sun. Small minnows glinted as they swam past in the water.

Seth and Pat dismounted and tied their horses to the OTV.

Liz watched Seth walk around the site, carefully checking the ground. He crouched low, seeing where the turtles had emerged from their underground nest. The tiny turtle tracks heading toward the stream. The imprint of the arrow striking the ground near where Johnathan's brother had sat was evident in the sand.

Seth took a thin branch and gently eased it into the hole the arrow had made. From the angle, he determined the direction of the shooter.

"We have to look for tracks in that direction," Seth said, pointing west, deeper into the park.

# Chapter Thirty-Six

Liz stopped the OTV in a clearing where she could launch the drone. It sent a video of the men riding along less accessible hunting trails that were not typically open to casual hikers. She sent the drone circling out ahead of them.

Seth pulled his horse up and jumped off to study the soft ground. Brushing pine needles aside, he found the imprint of a well-worn boot.

Pat joined him and tried to see what Seth saw, "This our guy?"

"Could be. It's fresh, not quite an hour old. He's not a heavy-weight, or the track would be deeper, and he's moving fast. See the space between this print and the next."

He showed the agent the spacing between the tracks. "Our man is not that tall either. Average height and slight build."

That was leaving out his cousin Zackery, who was five foot ten but weighed about two hundred pounds. He breathed a sigh of relief that he wouldn't have to arrest his cousin. But who would he be arresting?

His cell phone vibrated in his pocket, "Hold on a second."

"I'm here, Liz. What's up?" Seth put the phone on speaker so Pat could hear.

"The Sheriff is still with the parents, and they are not letting up. He also wanted us to know that he had received word that Malcolm Fletcher was released from the hospital yesterday. I know you and Pat wanted to ask him about the illegal orchids. Newsom is stonewalling and not saying much."

"Liz, ask the sheriff to find Fletcher, bring him in, and hold him for questioning. We'll talk to him as soon as we can." Pat said. "He knows more than he's letting on about the illegal orchid trade.

"Will do. Any news on your end?"

"We have some tracks we're following. Send the drone out ahead of us and see if you see anyone." Seth said.

They watched the drone buzz overhead and scooted away. The men mounted up and followed the trail left by the shooter. It was slow going. They had to stop and check for tracks often.

Seth looked around and checked his position. "Damn, this guy is smart. I hope we're not too late."

Pat hunched his shoulders, waiting for an explanation. "What?"

"It looks like we're being led back to Burns Lake Campground."

Seth called Liz. "Liz, get the drone over Burns Lake Campground. Hurry. See if you can spot our man with a bow. He'll be trying to get away. We're on our way there now."

Spurring the horses to a gallop, they raced to the campground.

Liz had the drone flying and chased a dark figure in camouflage carrying what could have been a crossbow. The figure was covered from head to foot. She couldn't see any details except that he wore a backpack and a ballcap.

Liz on the OTV and the men on horseback arrived in time to see a rusty white panel van speeding out of the parking lot, kicking up sand and gravel, obscuring the license plate.

They could only watch as the van disappeared in the distance.

# Chapter Thirty-Seven

Tired and dragging after unloading the horses at the Rez and thanking Seth's father, the two men entered the Sheriff's office.

Liz was already there exhausted, drinking a cold drink and talking to Deputy Franklin. She went to hug Seth but stopped short, "Whew, chief. You stink." Backing away, waving her hand in front of her face. If that's what riding a horse smells like, I might give it a pass."

"Aw, now, sweetheart. Is that any way to greet your brave warrior home from the hunt?" Seth smiled, grabbing his wife and kissing her soundly.

"Ew, not funny. Shower first, and then we'll see about after."

Everyone in the room burst out laughing at the exchange. Liz turned red as a beet and tried to hide behind Agent Miller.

"Oh God, you smell just as bad," Liz said. Sitting back down quickly.

Sheriff Woodson stood up with his hands on his hips, "If you three are done with the comedy act, we have some interrogating to do." He walked away, mumbling to himself.

Newsom was waiting for Seth and Agent Miller. His hands were cuffed to the table in front of him.

"I don't understand why I have to be handcuffed like this. Do you really think I can take the both of you on?"

"Professor Newsom, you have been read your rights. Are you

sure you don't want to call a lawyer?" Pat said.

"Look, I'm guilty of possessing orchids illegally. So fine me and let me go."

"Not so fast," Seth said. "You have collected ghost orchids from the National Preserve. That violates the Convention on International Trade in Endangered Species of Wild Fauna and Flora. That may require a fine and jail time. You will be brought before a judge."

Newsom was wide-eyed at this new revelation. Sweat began to bead on his brow. "You have got to be kidding me. It's all Bandaleri's fault. He brought me the orchids. I was only to hold them until he found a buyer. If I sold a little on the side, what did that matter? I was trying to propagate the ghost orchid, but I was not successful. I also tried with some of the other orchids and failed."

Seth rose and stretched. The FWC was responsible for enforcing the CITES Convention laws. The convention had 169 countries trying to protect their endangered plants and animals from illegal trafficking.

"Who connected you with Bandaleri?"

Newsom collapsed in his chair. "That little bastard Fletcher. He came to my home one evening. I was working in the greenhouse. He seemed interested in the orchids and what I was doing and asked if I had any luck selling them. At that time, I only had legal orchids. I'd cultivate my own or buy from farmer's markets or orchid shows.

It was a hobby. That was all.

"Fletcher asked if I'd like rare ones no one else had. He said there was a big market for them, and I could make a lot of money."

Newsom shook his empty soda can, closed his eyes, and breathed heavily. "I fell for it. At first, there were only a few plants. Then, more and more were delivered. I had to rent the storage unit to house them all."

Seth leaned against the wall and asked, "Didn't you try to get out of it?"

"Sure I did. I told Fletcher I wanted out. Then Bandaleri showed up with a couple of his thugs and threatened me. I was never so afraid in my life. Bandaleri said he had collectors waiting, and I was to keep my mouth shut and his supply chain going.”

Now, it was Agent Miller’s turn with the Professor.

“What about the other packages Bandaleri had you keep for him?”

“I didn’t ask. I didn’t want to know what was in them.”

# Chapter Thirty-Eight

"Let's talk about Agent Hernandez." Agent Miller said.

The professor turned white. His hands gripped the empty soda can.

"We found the trail cameras and reviewed the footage of you hitting Hernandez with a rock, knocking him to the ground. That could be an attempted murder charge."

"I wasn't thinking. The guy came up and said he was a federal agent and would report me for taking the ghost orchid. I had to stop him. If Bandaleri found out I had a ghost orchid, I don't know what he'd do. I wanted to try and propagate it for myself. Bandaleri would take all he could find in the preserve. That would be the end of the ghost orchid."

"The video shows you looking at someone or something right after you hit Hernandez. Can you tell us about that?"

Newsom relaxed a bit and started breathing again. "This big scruffy guy came from the direction of the oil rig. He was yelling something about Hernandez being a nosey government bastard and to stay out of his way or else."

Seth and Pat looked at each other. Seth nodded for Pat to follow him outside the room.

In the hallway, Seth told the agent about their discovery and the leak at the oil rig.

"After finding the repaired leak, Liz and I went to the oil refinery and met with the manager there, Nick Halleran. He has another guy, Sully, who fits Newsom's description roughly: six feet tall, two hundred pounds, and a bite. He could be meaner than a momma gator guarding her young. This Sully character and Halleran need to be questioned."

Pat paced up and down the short hallway. "There are a lot of interconnected pieces in the investigation. It's doing my head in."

"Put Newsom back in his cell for now. Let's see where Woodson is on tracking down Fletcher. I want to go home for a while, take a hot shower, eat, and go to bed."

"At least you have someone for you at home," Pat said, winking at Seth, poking at a sensitive spot.

Not taking the bait, Seth said, "I'm sure Janice Franklin would be more than happy to warm your bed if you asked nicely," with a sly grin.

"Tempting as that sounds, I don't like to mix business and pleasure." Pat stopped and raised his eyebrows, thinking. "Maybe when this is all over." Watching Janice walk away down the hall. "I'll have to think about that. On the other hand."

Seth rubbed a hand over his now beard-stubbled face. "I'll talk to Woodson before I leave about rounding up Fletcher. He can't be that hard to find."

"I'm wondering what kind of connections Bandaleri has that enable him to bring in so many illegal orchids. Miami International Airport would be the most logical, but Customs and Border Protection is pretty stiff when it comes to plants coming into the country," Pat said.

"It's got to be another smaller airport without the tight security. I'll put Liz on it tonight."

Seth saw Sheriff Woodson sitting in his office and knocked on the door. "Any word on Malcolm Fletcher?"

"I'm sending deputies out to the University tomorrow. Fletcher was not at his listed address today. We might find him somewhere on campus."

"Thanks, keep me posted. Oh, Fletcher had a sticker on his backpack that said "Straight Arrow Archery." I think he might be a member there."

"Good, I'll have deputies check there as well."

# Chapter Thirty-Nine

Nickosi greeted Seth with wags and big slobbery kisses. "I guess you missed me."

"I missed you too," Liz said, throwing her arms around him and kissing him passionately. "That's just a preview of what's to come later, but you still stink and need a shower."

"Mmm, I can't wait."

Following her into the Kitchen, he lifted the lid from a pot on the stove and found a simmering chili.

"Go take that shower, and I'll make some cornbread."

"After supper, I've got some research for you to do. I'll tell you all about it later."

Seth's phone rang just as the corn muffins came out of the oven.

Liz dropped the pan on the counter and grabbed the phone. "Hello. Hold on, I'll get him."

Wrapping a towel around himself, Seth took the phone. Liz sat on the edge of their bed and waited.

"That was Pat. Come on, I'll explain while we eat." Seth dressed quickly in jeans and a tee shirt and followed Liz to the kitchen.

Over their supper, Seth told her what they had found out about Newsom, Fletcher, and Bandaleri.

"We think they have to use one of the smaller airports to bring in the illegal orchids from South America and Asia. That's the only way to avoid Customs and Border patrols. We're hoping you can research and find a couple likely ones to check out."

"I can do that. By the way, your father called. There is a meeting on the Miccosukee Reservation regarding the potential designation of part of the park as a wilderness area. He thought you might want to be there."

"Yeah, I do. I want to see who's there as well as hear the issues. I know that Zackery and the cousins will probably be there."

Liz figured she could call and set up a family supper with Rowena before the meeting. She loved having her new family around; any excuse to get them together was a welcome opportunity.

Seth dozed on the couch with Nickosi on the floor in front of him while Liz searched on the computer for possible airports.

She was surprised to find three pages of small to medium airports in the Southwest region of Florida. Leaning back in her chair, she realized there were only two ways to get illegal contraband into South Florida: by boat or plane. Drug smugglers used both ways, and the border patrols had their hands full trying to catch them.

Liz noticed the Seminoles had an airport right on the Big Cypress Reservation. She'd have to ask Seth about that.

Thinking about possible small airports that the illegal orchid importers could use, she crossed off all the small, privately owned ones, as well as those connected to hospitals, training facilities, and even a counter-terrorism training center.

Looking over at Seth, who was sleeping peacefully, she yawned and stretched. *I'll think about this again in the morning. My brain is tired.*

"Come on, Nickosi, you need to go out before I go to bed." Nudging the dog with her foot.

Liz stood on the porch, waiting for the dog to do his thing. Warm, strong arms slid around her waist, drawing her back into him.

"I was trying not to wake you."

"I was half awake anyway. I seem to remember you promised me something, and I mean to collect it."

"Oh, do you now," Liz said, gliding around to face him. Well, I always deliver on my promises." kissing him deeply. "That's a down payment. You better come and collect the rest.

"Come on, Nickosi, I've a debt to collect."

# Chapter Forty

The alarm sounded at 6:30 am. Nickosi bounded onto the bed, squeezing his massive body between Seth and Liz. He pushed Seth out with his paws and sprawled out to take his place.

"Thanks a lot, pal," he said, rolling his shoulders and heading for the bathroom.

Liz was already in the kitchen, and coffee was brewing when he came out. "I'm going to call Sheriff Woodson later and see if he managed to locate Malcolm Fletcher." She said, placing a steaming cup in front of him.

"I also want to talk to Nick Halleran and his man Sully," Seth said.

"Pat might want to be in on that one."

Seth's phone rang, making Nickosi's ears perk up.

"Whose calling at this hour?" Looking at the caller ID, he muttered, "Shit, what now?" Taking his coffee and the phone outside, Seth sat on the porch while he talked to Sheriff Woodson.

After a few minutes, he came in, shaking his head. "Get a move on. Our arrow shooter has struck again. Remember that homeless guy?"

"Yeah, his name was Max Weller of no fixed abode. He was quite a character."

"Someone shot an arrow through his tent last night and almost hit him. Weller called the sheriff and was screaming that somebody was trying to kill him."

"How did he get out of jail, and why would anyone want to kill Max Weller? He's a harmless old wanderer looking for a place to roost for a while."

"Why he's not in jail is beyond me," Seth said. "He must have posted bail somehow."

Liz remembered that Weller had been cautioned for picking palmetto berries, which was against the law. Could that be the reason he was targeted?

# Chapter Forty-One

Dressing quickly, Liz and Seth drove to the campsite where Weller had set up his new campsite.

There, they met up with Sheriff Woodson, Deputy Franklin, and a very agitated Max Weller.

"I want restitution for the damage to my property. I can't afford to buy a new tent. That crazy lunatic destroyed my tent, my living quarters. Where am I supposed to live?" Weller held up his tent and poked his hand through the hole in his tent where the arrow had ripped through.

"If I hadn't reached for my flashlight, that arrow woulda gone right here." Weller pointed to the middle of his chest.

"I was afraid our shooter was going to escalate things. We have to do more to catch this son of a bitch." Woodson said.

Looking at Weller, he said, "If you hadn't been poaching palmetto berries, he wouldn't have shot at you in the first place."

"Yeah, like I said. A man has to earn a living."

Seth stared at the ground and tried to think of some way to catch the shooter. The shooter targeted people he thought were harming the environment or breaking the rules. Perhaps the best way was to arrange something to bring the shooter to us. He'd have to come up with a plan.

Woodson interrupted his thinking, "Mr. Weller, Deputy Franklin will bring you by my office, and we can see what we can do about getting you a new tent."

Weller humphed and began to gather his things. Deputy Franklin scrunched up her face over the thought of having a smelly vagrant in her car, but orders were orders.

Seth shared his thoughts with the Sheriff, "Sheriff, we have to set up a way to bring the shooter to us. Trying to track him after he strikes is a waste of resources. I'm sure we can put our heads together and come up with something."

"You're right. Can you come by my office later to discuss it?"

"Sure, We'll be there. I'll call when we're on our way."

Seth and Liz still had to make their rounds of the campgrounds and fishing spots in the preserve. They were near the Monument Lake Campground and not far from Eleven Mile Road and the OTV trails out that way.

"There's an airport right where Eleven Mile Road meets State Road 41. It sits on the border between Collier County and Dade County. It's a training facility for some of the big airlines. I remember reading about it. It's a public facility but only has one runway. How about we check it out? Could it be our orchid smugglers are using it? What do you think?" Liz said.

"Let's do it. We'll have to make it quick so we can meet up with Woodson later."

There wasn't much to see when they drove in, and there were no hangers or warehouses. The facility covered twenty-four thousand-plus acres and was eerily quiet. Buzzards circled overhead, riding the thermals as a pair of sandhill cranes strutted slowly across the runway. It could have been a scene from a Stephen King movie.

Seth drove their OTV slowly toward the only building along the runway. It apparently housed the facility's operations, such as communications and electricity.

Alongside the building, Seth noticed fresh tire tracks. "These aren't that old. Maybe only a day or two. Someone has used this airport recently."

"I think whoever used it didn't file a flight plan to land here. I never asked if Bandaleri got bailed out and when."

Seth took out his phone and called Sheriff Woodson. "We'll be on our way shortly. We're checking out the Dade-Collier Training and Transition Airport. We may have spotted something. Can you tell us if Bandaleri made bail and when?"

"I'll have to check and let you know when you get here. In the meantime, I'm trying to find Fletcher. He's gone to ground somewhere."

Seth was quiet on the way to see Sheriff Woodson.

Liz could almost hear the gears turning in his head. She knew he was trying to figure out a way to bring the shooter out in the open.

Pulling into the Collier County Sheriff's Parking lot, they spotted Agent Pat Miller's car.

"I wonder what he's up to," Seth grimaced. As much as he liked the guy on another level, he wished the agent would stay in D.C. anywhere but around his wife.

# Chapter Forty-Two

The talk in the room stopped as Seth and Liz entered. "Hey, every-one. Care to catch us up." Liz said, noticing Deputy Franklin was sitting close to Pat.

"We still haven't found Fletcher," Woodson said.

"Nick Halleran is coming in tomorrow with his manager. We don't have anything concrete that ties him to the murder of Agent Hernandez except that boot print near the drill head," Pat said.

Seth tapped his fingers on the table, "Wait, in the video, Newsom stopped and looked at something or someone before he took off. What if he saw that guy, Sully? If the professor could ID him, we would have an eyewitness that he was there when Hernandez was murdered."

Liz jumped up and kissed Seth on the cheek. "You are brilliant. None of us thought of that."

Seth was tired and wanted to discuss the reason he was there. "We were going to talk about drawing the arrow shooter out. He seems to strike at random, but usually where he can make a quick getaway along SR 41. He's fast, on foot when he strikes, and has a van. We need deputies at the parking lots to be on the lookout for that van."

Woodson spread out a map of the Big Cypress Preserve on the table. Seth stood to circle the Burns Lake, Monument, and Eleven Mile Road sites. "We know he has used these spots before, and I'm confident he will again. The shooter knows these trails. He proved it when we were chasing him with the horses."

Pat clapped Seth on the shoulder. "That's a start. Now, we only need the bait. I think I have a plan for that. He's an eco-warrior. We leak to the news stations that we are bringing in a suspect in connection with the murder of a Federal Agent who was investigating an oil leak in the Big Cypress National Preserve."

Everyone was silent, digesting what Pat said.

"Only if Halleran and his man wear a vest. I don't want them killed by this nut case." Woodson said.

"That can be arranged. I'll leak to the news and be here first thing in the morning."

"You have a place to stay tonight?" Woodson asked the agent.

Pat looked sideways at Deputy Franklin. "Yeah, I do."

Franklin put her head down and blushed as others looked her way.

Liz remembered the airport and wanted to share her thoughts with the Sheriff. "Before we go, I wanted to tell you about the Collier-Dade Airport. Seth and I believe it's where the illegal orchids are coming in, and we found fresh tire tracks beside the operations building. It's an unmanned public operation."

"I did check, and Bandaleri was bailed out almost immediately. I don't have the manpower to go after the shooter and a bail jumper at the same time. Bandaleri will have to wait," Woodson said

Liz understood but was disappointed at the same time. Maybe she could come up with something on her own. Unfortunately, she could not go undercover this time because Bandaleri knew her. An idea began to percolate in her brain, but would Seth go along with it?

The group broke up, with each heading their own way. Pat waved as he climbed into Janice's car.

"Guess he didn't wait after all," Seth said, waving back.

# Chapter Forty-Three

Zackery was sitting on the steps when Seth and Liz arrived home. Immediately, they panicked, thinking something had happened to Seth's mom or dad.

"What's wrong? Where's Mom and Dad? Are they ok?" Seth said, leaping from the truck. Usually, his parents watched Nickosi when they were on duty or expected to be gone, and the dog needed to be fed or let out.

"Whoa, there, cousin. They are fine. I let them off the hook and took care of the furry one. You mentioned that you might be interested in attending one of the meetings about designating part of the preserve as a wilderness area. There is one tomorrow evening on the Miccosukee Rez. You should come if you want to know what is happening and what is at stake for our people."

Zackery sat with Nickosi's big head in his lap, rubbing the dog behind his ears. The dog was in heaven with the attention.

Seth didn't hesitate, "Yes, this is important to our people. I'm living here now and need to be more involved. Are Mom and Dad going?"

"Try and stop them. Dad is one of the speakers."

"I'll be there. Can Liz come?" Sometimes, outsiders were not welcome.

"She's Seminole now, too." Zackery stood to leave. Nickosi looked at him with sad eyes.

Seth and Zackery bumped fists, "Save us a seat."

Liz waved goodbye quickly and raced up the steps and into the house to call Rowena.

Liz handed the phone to Seth when he walked in the door. "Your Dad wants to talk to you."

His dad told him how pleased he was that Seth wanted to come to the meeting tomorrow evening and that he was interested in his tribe's affairs after living in the white man's world for so long.

Andres believed the old ways were the best, and even though he supported his son's decisions, he always wanted him to live as a Seminole.

Rowena took the phone from her husband and told her son how pleased she was to have them to supper before the meeting the next day and that she would prepare something special for them.

Seth hung up and rolled his eyes at Liz, "I can see your hand in this."

"Whatever do you mean?" Liz said, pretending to be innocent.

"You and my mother are planning the little get-together before tomorrow's meeting."

"I like your family and want to spend time with them. I thought it was a good excuse to get together since we will end up at the same place eventually." She said, raising her shoulders and making a funny face. What she wasn't telling was that she wanted to ask for help with her plan to catch the importers of the illegal orchids. The ghost orchid in the preserve was not the only orchid that needed protection.

Seth enveloped her in his arms. "You're amazing. I'm so lucky that you came into my life."

She pushed back to look into his gray-green eyes. "I'm the lucky one, Chief. I have everything I could ever want with you: a family that accepts me, a job I love. What more could I ask for."

At that moment, they both had the same fleeting thought. One that had never crossed their minds before. An unspoken thought. Were they ready to talk about starting a family of their own? Not tonight, another time.

Nickosi whined at the door. He needed to go out. The moment and the thought vanished.

# Chapter Forty-Four

The parking lot was already packed when they arrived, and people were streaming in to voice their opinion on the proposal to turn large sections of the Big Cypress Preserve into a wilderness area.

Luckily, Seth's family had saved them two seats near the front.

Several prominent members of the Miccosukee and Seminole tribes took their turns speaking before the group.

A petition signed by 25,000 members of the two tribes was presented to Congress to outline their concerns. Seth's father stood reading part of an article from the Miami Herald, which stated, "It makes it almost impossible to develop the land — which both sides generally support — but also blocks or puts hefty permit requirements in front of things that have been done for decades in the Big Cypress, everything from hunting, riding off-road vehicles or giving airboat tours. Organizations like the National Parks Conservation Association have long supported wilderness designation in Big Cypress. They consider it a powerful tool to slow down oil drilling and hold oil explorers on the land to a higher standard for repairing the damage they left."

He paused to take a breath and let the words sink in. "We all want access to our ancestral lands. We want to be able to hold our ceremonies, hunt, and fish, and collect our plants and herbs as we have always done. How to protect the land for future generations and allow us access will be a compromise on both sides."

Next to speak was a member from the Izaak Walton League of Gladesmen. These men have hunted and recreated in the Big Cypress for generations. They feared they would be effectively locked out of the land they had used for hundreds of years.

Seth listened carefully to each speaker and could see both sides of the argument, but in the end, there was no clear winner. There had to be a way to stop developers and oil companies while still allowing the tribe and Gladesmen access.

Someone handed out articles reprinted from the newspapers and a list of people in the Senate and Congress to contact. The only way was to make their voices heard. Maybe someone would listen.

The meeting was breaking up, and Liz was looking for Zackery. She had to speak to him about her plan to catch the orchid smugglers and enlist his help.

"Who are you looking for?" Seth asked, noticing her worried look as she scanned the departing crowd.

"I wanted to say goodbye to your mom and dad." She was becoming quite skilled at telling little white lies.

"They're talking to Zackery and the others in the doorway. Come on, and we can catch them."

They pushed through groups of people still talking about the meeting or catching up with friends.

"Mom, Dad, I'm glad we came tonight. There is a lot at stake we didn't know about."

"It's a sensitive issue. I'm happy to see you take an interest." Andres said. "Come walk with me to my car."

Liz raised an eyebrow and made a face to see Andres take Seth away.

"Not to worry. It's tribal business," Rowena said, patting Liz's arm. Andres is considering stepping down from the tribal council and wants Seth to take his place. The council needs young blood with new ideas. The council may object because Seth has not lived as a Seminole for many years, but the place is his by right.

Liz was stunned and didn't know what to say. She had no idea what the rules were in such a situation.

She blew out her breath. All thoughts of Zackery flew out of her mind. "What would it mean to have Seth on the tribal council?

"Thanks for the heads-up, Rowena. I appreciate it." She hugged her mother-in-law and, hooking arms, walked out to join the men in the parking lot.

# Chapter Forty-Five

Liz woke to the smell of coffee and the sound of the TV news. Rolling over, she threw off the covers and walked down the hall to find Seth, coffee in hand, watching the news channel.

"What's got you up at this time? The alarm isn't due for another hour." She said, rubbing the sleep from her eyes and yawning.

"I couldn't sleep. I wanted to hear the leaked news that was supposed to draw the shooter out."

"You think the news will put it out this early?"

"I hope so. We need to get our people in place."

Liz padded barefoot to the kitchen, where she got a cup of coffee. After settling down, curling her feet under her, she reached for a blanket to ward off the morning chill nestling near Seth.

"Hold on, here it is," Seth said, increasing the volume.

The announcer detailed that two men were being brought into the Naples Sheriff's office later that day to answer questions in regards to the death of Federal Agent Adam Hernandez. The men are connected with the oil refining plant at Raccoon Point, near where the agent's body was found. The sheriff's deputies will escort them from the plant to the Naples office. We have been told to expect this to happen around 11 o'clock this morning. Please tune in for the latest news as it unfolds. From there, the channel flipped to the weather.

Seth relaxed and said, "Let's hope that brings out the shooter."

"It certainly said all the right things. I hope Woodson is putting a vest on Halleran and that guy Sully, just in case."

"I think we better get going and make sure everything is in place."

It took them a few minutes to get dressed and wash up the few breakfast dishes. Liz opened the door to let Nickosi out and found Agent Miller standing there, hand raised, ready to knock.

"You're early," Liz said with a look of surprise.

"I figured you'd be up. Did you see the news this morning?"

"Come in," Liz said, stepping aside to let him pass. "Yes, we did. Seth was up at the crack of dawn waiting for it. It didn't name Nick Halleran or Jack Sullivan. We don't want a lawsuit on our hands."

Seth came down the hall, tucking in his shirt, "Hi Pat. You're up with the birds. I guess you saw the news. We're on our way to the sheriff's office."

"That's where I'm headed, but I wanted to go over a couple of things. Since you found Agent Hernandez and the first arrow, who have you come across who has had access to a crossbow?"

"Shit, Pat, that could be a pretty long list. There's my cousins for starts. Lucas and Monica Osceola have a crossbow. Malcolm Fletcher shoots at the Straight Arrow archery club. Any member of that club could own a crossbow. It could be anyone on the rez or one of a hundred hunters in the area. There were a lot of people at the meeting last night. Any one of them could own a crossbow."

Pat stretched his long legs out in front of him as he sat in the kitchen, scratching Nickosi behind the dog's ears.

"I heard about the meeting. It's a sore subject on both sides."

Seth's phone rang. "Hold on. It's Woodson."

He listened for a minute, shook his head, and turned, "You're not going to believe this. "Nick Halleran was hurt on his way to work this morning. He was shot by an arrow as he stepped out of his truck at the Raccoon Point Plant. He's in surgery now."

Stunned silence filled the room.

# Chapter Forty-Six

The sheriff's station was in chaos when they walked in. Phones were ringing, and deputies were running about like scared rabbits.

Sheriff Woodson could be heard shouting in his office through the closed door. "How in hell can something like this happen? I'll have someone's head for this."

Deputy Franklin eased herself out of the office and leaned back against the door. Eyes wide, she said, "I'd be careful. He's after whoever's responsible for shooting Nick Halleran with an arrow. The news leak was released much earlier than expected. It wasn't supposed to go out until 9 o'clock."

"Damn, I heard it at 5 o'clock. That gave the shooter a four-hour head start on us." Seth said.

Agent Miller stood thoughtful, "We can still bring in Jack Sullivan on schedule."

"And we get a vest on the guy so he doesn't suffer the same fate as his boss. Maybe Newsom can ID him as being at the scene when Hernandez was murdered. That would clear the professor," Liz said.

They looked through the window into the Sheriff's office and saw him pacing and running his hands through his sparse hair.

Seth got brave and knocked before opening the door, "Is it safe to come in?"

"Yes, damn it. I called the TV station, and they said some bastard there had decided to run the leak early to fill a space. I told them that it caused an innocent man to be murdered, and they promised to, and I quote, "look into it." I've had everyone from the governor on down shouting at me this morning about the cockup over this. I'm not happy that we got someone killed trying to catch this nutcase."

Agent Miller, standing behind Seth, said, trying to reassure the Sheriff, "We will catch him today. We have to. Are you sure Jack Sullivan is going to be at the refinery?"

"He better be. I left two deputies there to sit on him. He's the one who found Halleran and reported it. Sullivan was pretty shaken up and wanted to leave. I convinced him to stay, and the deputies are there for his protection."

"I have some questions for Professor Newsom about the orchid and importers. Will I be able to speak to him at some point?" Liz asked. She still wanted to catch who was illegally importing endangered and protected orchids.

"We need him to ID Sullivan, so we'll bring him in. God, I wish I'd stayed in bed today." Woodson said, taking a seat behind his desk and rubbing his face.

"Shit, I hate today," Woodson got up and went out to the main room. "Listen up. I want everyone to get the hell out here and be on alert. We know the last time the shooter got away in a white panel van. He may or may not use the same vehicle.

"I have divided you all into units. Deputy Franklin is handing out the assignments. There is a map of the preserve. We will bring the suspect down Eleven Mile Rd from the Raccoon Point Plant. Units will cover Monument Lake and Burns Lake Campsites along SR 41.

"There is a Florida trail running from SR 41 to I-75. Deputies Grayson and Corday will cover that on OTV. Agent Miller will have a drone in the air to help track the shooter. Keep your eyes open. We have to get him this time."

Seth looked at the time. "We better get moving. I don't want to be late to the party." Outside, the OTV was already on the trailer attached to the truck.

Deputies streamed out of the building into patrol cars. Sheriff Woodson and Deputy Franklin took off for the refinery at Raccoon Point.

In a far corner of the parking lot was an older-model pickup covered with mud and debris. Scrunched down in the driver's seat was a man just as scruffy as the truck. Beside him on the passenger seat was a crossbow loaded with arrows. He chuckled to himself, watching.

# Chapter Forty-Seven

Agent Miller tucked his vehicle into the pines and scrub brush at the end of Eleven Mile Rd. He carried his drone equipment the rest of the way up the trail to where the oil rig creaked up and down, pumping the black sludge from the earth.

He figured this was a good spot to launch the drone when the time came. There was at least two hours before they were due to move Sullivan to the sheriff's station. Finding a comfortable spot under a cypress tree, the agent sat and waited.

# Chapter Forty-Eight

S eth and Liz took the OTV off the trailer and stowed their supplies. "I'd rather be on horseback for this. It would do less damage to the trail," Seth said.

"I'll take my horsepower with four wheels, thank you very much." Liz scoffed.

"When this is over, I'll get you on a horse, and you'll see how much you'll enjoy it."

"Yeah, right."

They watched as the sheriff's unmarked vehicles arrived and tried to blend in with the other cars and camper vans in the campsite.

Sheriff Woodson arrived, nodding as he drove past."

" This better go as planned, and we get this idiot. Woodson has a lot of manpower invested in this today. After yesterday, his job is on the line." Seth said.

Liz opened a bottle of water for each of them and settled back to wait. The Sheriff was to call them when he left the plant with Sullivan.

Seth scanned the area and didn't see any sign of a white panel van. The only thing that struck him was a filthy mud-caked pickup at the edge of the Monument Lake Campground.

He nudged Liz, drawing her attention to it. "The only thing holding that heap together is the mud."

They both laughed at the joke. But something in the back of

Seth's mind was tingling. Did he see that truck before? But where?

The pickup's owner was half a mile away, walking towards Raccoon Point. He was on a mission and didn't intend on getting caught anytime soon. He was pissed at himself for not finishing off Halleran as he planned.

# Chapter Forty-Nine

Sheriff Woodson met Pat at the oil rig after they left their vehicles behind, where Eleven Mile Road ended.

"You ready to put that thing up?"

"Just say the word." Pat opened the case containing the drone to show the sheriff.

"That's pretty impressive. I sure hope it does the trick. Seth and Liz are waiting at the bottom of the trail, ready to go."

Pat was assembling the drone and turning on the electronics. "Let's do this."

The sheriff and his men carried on up the trail to the plant.

Waiting outside were the two deputies he left to guard Jack Sullivan. "He still inside?"

"Yeah, and madder'n a wet hen, sir," A young rookie said.

As soon as the Sheriff opened the door, Sullivan shouted, "What the hell is going on? Halleran gets hurt, and now you're holding me prisoner?"

"It was for your protection. We are going to take you to the Naples Sheriff's office." Woodson handed Sullivan a bulletproof vest to wear.

"You've got to be kidding. You really think this is necessary?" Sullivan said, holding up the heavy vest in front of him.

"Look, do you want to end up like Halleran or not? Your choice. I'll just put it in the report that you refused to wear the vest and were apprised of the risk."

Sullivan grumbled but put on the vest.

"Hey, I've got a lot of questions. Like, what are you doing to catch whoever shot my boss with a fuckin arrow?"

"That's what we're trying to do. We don't want you to be his next victim."

That seemed to calm Sullivan down a bit. Woodson opened the office door and stepped out into the rising Florida heat. It was like a sauna. The humidity was palpable. Before long, everyone was drenched in sweat and clothing stuck to their skin.

Woodson had some deputies fan out while he and Deputy Franklin walked with Sullivan to where they had left their vehicles.

Nerves were on edge as they walked the few hundred yards to the drill rig.

Agent Miller was ready with his drone and shrugged his shoulders. "What's up, Sheriff?"

"Just keep your radio on in case. We're not home free yet."

The group walked on, tension building, waiting for the shooter to strike. Every rustle in the trees and underbrush made someone stop and look.

Finally, Woodson saw his vehicle. He was looking forward to turning on the A/C and cooling down.

"Son of a bitch," Woodson shouted when he got closer. "That fuck'n bastard. He's playing with us."

An arrow stuck out of the grill of the Sheriff's vehicle. The heavy-duty arrow had penetrated the radiator, and all the water and coolant were now on the ground.

Sullivan held back a chuckle. Even Franklin wanted to laugh but didn't dare.

Woodson shoved Sullivan at Franklin. "Get him to the station."

Woodson ordered the remaining deputies to pack up and return to the station.

He leaned against his disabled vehicle, removed his hat, and wiped the sweat off his brow. His face was like thunder, and he was more determined than ever to catch the shooter.

# Chapter Fifty

Seth got the call from Woodson to pack up. The message was short, and he could tell something wasn't right.

"Did he know what happened?" Liz asked, returning to the truck after getting the OTV back on the trailer and stowing their gear.

"No, but he sounded pissed at something or someone. I guess we'll find out back at the station."

As Seth started the engine, a man ran out in front of him. "You've got to help. A snake bit my wife."

"Did you see the snake?" Liz said, reaching for the first aid kit.

"No, but my wife did, and she has two holes in her leg. Hurry, please."

They got the OTV back off the trailer, and the man directed them to where he had left his wife on the trail.

She was sitting on a fallen log, crying and in pain from the bite.

"Have you called the ambulance?" Seth asked.

"They are on the way but said it will take twenty minutes."

"We can take your wife to the trailhead. That will cut down on the time."

Liz looked at the bite. There were two small holes above her right ankle. "Hi, I'm Officer Corday. What's your name?"

"I'm Judith, Judith Rankle. I was walking along and felt a sharp jab. I looked down and saw this snake going into the brush."

"Can you describe the snake for me? It would really help,"

Liz said, trying to calm the woman.

"It was small but fat, only about this long." The woman held out her hands to measure approximately twenty-four inches.

"What color was it?'

The woman crunched her eyes, trying to remember. "It was dark gray and had reddish blotches running down its back."

"A pygmy rattler bit you. They are venomous, and you'll need to go to the hospital. You will not die, but there will be swelling and soreness. It won't be pleasant for a while. They only bite when they feel threatened or you step too close."

Liz wrapped the site and helped get Judith and her husband on the OTV. Bouncing back down the trail, they heard the ambulance coming.

The transfer to the ambulance went smoothly. Mr. Ranklin went with his wife to the hospital, repeatedly expressing his gratitude for the FWC officers' assistance.

Seth looked at the OTV and the trailer. "Let's hope this is the last time." Getting the OTV loaded and unloaded in the heat was exhausting work. "Come on, let's do this. One more time."

Turning the A/C up full blast, Liz leaned back. "I'm glad that bite was only a pygmy, not a big Eastern diamondback rattler. She would be in big trouble if it were."

"You got that right. I want to know what got Woodson all steamed up. After we check in at the station, I want to drop by and talk to my father about being on the Seminole Council. I've been thinking about it."

"Whatever you decide, Chief is ok with me," Liz said, reaching over to squeeze his hand. She wasn't feeling too well after dealing with the OTV.

"I do want to talk with Newsom about the orchids. He has to know more than he's saying." Liz continued.

Pulling into the station, they saw Deputy Franklin standing outside with a couple other deputies. "You might not want to go in there. The Sheriff is ready to bite everyone's head off."

"What happened? He just told us to pack up and sounded pissed off." Seth said.

"The shooter didn't go after Sullivan. The guy only shot an arrow into the Sheriff's radiator, disabling it. The Sheriff went ballistic."

Liz cringed, knowing how Woodson had counted on catching the shooter and all the manpower and planning he had put into it.

"Do you know if they brought Newsom in for questioning?" Liz asked.

"Yeah, he's there," Franklin said.

"Any word on finding Malcolm Fletcher?" Seth asked.

"He's still in the wind and the number one suspect for being the shooter."

# Chapter Fifty-One

Liz sat across the scarred table from Professor Newsom. The man appeared to have aged ten years in the few days he had been in jail. "It's not fair keeping me in jail. I have rights."

"You were trafficking in endangered species. That's against the International CITES agreement. That's a big law to break. You have a bail hearing coming up. If you cooperate, that could go a long way toward helping you out."

"Whatever you want. I have to get out of here." Newsom pleaded, rattling the cuffs on his wrists.

"Tell me who is bringing the orchids into the country."

"I don't know. Bandaleri knows all that." Newsom said, whimpering. He feared that his chances of getting out would be slim if he didn't supply some answers. Unfortunately, he knew next to nothing.

"How did you contact Bandaleri?"

"He contacted me the first time. I saw an ad in an orchid fanciers magazine for one-of-a-kind exotic orchids. I left my contact information, and Bandaleri called me, saying he could supply me with rare orchids if I would agree to house some for collectors and fulfill other miscellaneous requests. Stupid me, I jumped at the chance. It didn't occur to me at the time that I was doing anything illegal."

"Do you know how the orchids were coming into the country?"

"That I do know. Bandaleri let it slip that he had to meet a plane to pick up a delivery. He had to give his man directions, and he must have thought I wasn't listening."

Liz was waiting for information on when and where the plane was landing. Then, she could make her plan to intercept it.

She saw Newsom hesitate. "Ok, where is the airport?" Liz could see Newsom looking for a way out for himself. He'd said too much without any gain.

"Before I do, I want a lawyer, and I want to make a deal. A proper deal on paper."

"You have got to be kidding me," Liz jumped up and threw her coffee cup across the room.

She banged on the door and shouted at the deputy who opened it. "Get this idiot a lawyer," she rolled her shoulders and tried to calm down.

The room was quiet as the deputies watched her walk out. The only one brave enough to approach her was Seth.

"I take it didn't go well."

"No, he lawyered up. Someone must have gotten to him and told him to keep his mouth shut."

Liz stopped a young deputy and asked her to obtain a defense attorney for Newsom as soon as possible. "Let me know when Newsom is ready to talk again."

"It's getting late. Let's go see my folks." Seth said. "My mom will feed us, and I can talk with my father about being on the council. I want to know what's involved before I agree to anything."

# Chapter Fifty-Two

They swung by their house and picked up Nickosi. The dog jumped in the truck, taking up the whole back seat.

It was a short drive to the Big Cypress Reservation. As they drew closer, Nickosi knew where they were going and became even more excited. He loved visiting Rowena and Andres because he got spoiled like any grandchild would.

Seth pulled in behind Zackery's truck. The smell of something on the grill wafted on the breeze.

Rowena came out carrying fresh corn on the cob. "You're right on time. Zackery brought some deer steaks. I've got baked potatoes and corn. There's strawberry rhubarb pie for later."

Liz leaned into Seth. "I've never had deer before. What does it taste like?" she whispered, not wanting to offend his family.

"Try a bit. Put some sauce on it. If you don't like it, don't worry. Not everyone does."

Liz helped Rowena set the table and watched Andres cook the deer steaks. She didn't mention that she had never had deer before. There were many things she was experiencing for the first time now that they were living closer to Seth's family. A loving family unit was one of them.

Zackery discussed hunting on the preserve with Seth and the changes the government wanted to implement. He had to understand what the change in making part of the preserve a wilderness would mean to his people and the Miccosukee.

Zackery was smart. He studied agriculture and plant medicine at the University of Florida.

Seth wondered why his father didn't ask Zackery to take his place on the tribal council.

"Zackery, my father has spoken to me about taking his place on the tribal council. I'm kinda surprised he didn't ask you."

"When he mentioned stepping down, I told him I wasn't interested. I like fighting from the outside. You know, no rules. I'm interested in tribal issues, but more specifically in what's happening to the land, such as in the preserve. I can organize petitions and talk to the Gladesmen and other groups. I represent everyone and not one group."

"I understand." Seth could see Zackery's point. He became a wildlife officer to protect the environment and nature. He had a lot in common with his cousin. A lot more than he thought.

Andres came over, offering cold beers. "We'll eat soon." Looking at Seth, he asked, " You given any more thought to taking my place on the council?"

"Liz and I talked and have questions. I have a demanding job, which means I'm not always available. If I take the position, I want to do it right."

"The council meets once a month. Tribal members submit topics they would like to discuss. We allocate funds, settle disputes, and handle other administrative tasks. Once in a while, something like what is happening with the preserve occurs. The council also strives to help organize community events, such as the rodeo or ceremonies, to keep our culture alive. We have to teach the younger generation our traditions."

"Would you believe they have me teaching the high school kids a course on herbal medicine?" Zackery laughed.

"That's right. The council approved that last year." Andres said.

Liz was standing nearby and heard what Andres was saying. She went to Rowena. "Do you think Seth should take the council position? How much time does it take? I know he wants to please his father, but you know what his job is like."

"It's not that bad. If Seth has to miss a meeting, they will carry on without him. Andres wants him to be more involved in the tribal business and traditions. That's all. If he decides not to take it, his father will be disappointed, but he'll get over it."

Liz looked at the men and thought how lucky she was to have found such a loving and supportive family.

"Hey, we're gonna eat tonight before the mosquitoes eat us alive," Rowena called. She had set out citronella candles to help keep the insects away. The sun was setting; soon, even the candles would lose the battle.

Taking their seats, Seth took Liz's hand and looked her in the eyes. She nodded. "You can do this, Chief."

"I guess I'll take the council position," Seth said, letting out a deep breath.

He brought her hand to his lips. Liz was not the only one who was lucky.

# Chapter Fifty-Three

Newsom and his lawyer were ready and waiting the following day.

Liz tackled them alone while Seth went to patrol the campsites in the preserves.

Entering the room, she was surprised to see a smart-looking young Latino woman sitting with Professor Newsom in the interrogation room. She expected a scruffy, frayed-collar intern.

Reaching across the table, Liz introduced herself, "I'm Officer Corday."

The woman responded coolly, "I'm Maria Ortiz. I have been hired as Professor Newsom's attorney."

Hired, Liz wondered. Who was footing the bill for her services?

"Professor Newsom and I have spoken. Apparently, you believe he has information that you need to apprehend some criminals who are in breach of the CITIES agreement. Am I correct?"

Miss Ortiz's language was formal and unsettling. Liz knew she was someone to be wary of.

"Yes. The professor said he could give me more information if we provided him with a lawyer, and here you are."

However, the mystery was how he had hired a high-priced attorney in a designer suit overnight.

"Agreed. The professor will provide the airport's name in exchange for all charges against him to be dropped." Miss Otiz smiled, revealing perfect white teeth that reminded Liz of a predatory shark.

"After all, he was duped, persuaded, naively to house the orchids for the traffickers. He didn't realize at the time that he was breaking any laws."

Liz could almost see how that would play out before a jury. A university professor, enthralled by collecting exotic orchids, was given the opportunity to collect rare orchids from around the world. The FWC would lose the case.

"I'll have to run it up the chain of command and see what they say." Liz stood and left the room. There had been no mention of the other packages or what they might have contained. She planned to let that go for now.

A decision on this scale was too big to make on her own. She made a call to the Florida Fish and Wildlife Conservation Commission (FWC) headquarters. They would have to make the decision. She hoped it would not take too long. Sometimes, these cases could drag on for weeks, months, or years.

She stopped by Sheriff Woodson's office to brief him and let him know that Newsom had seen his lawyer.

"Yeah, I saw her. That was no court-appointed attorney. I expect him to be bailed out here pretty soon, too."

By the way, Halleran made it through surgery. The arrow missed all the vital organs, and he'll be able to go back to work. Right now, he's screaming his head off to anyone who will listen about how we are letting a maniac run around lose trying to kill people.

"That figures," Liz said, perching on the edge of Woodson's desk. "As for Newsom, someone is pulling the strings there. I'm betting it's Bandaleri. The professor knows something he doesn't want us to know."

"Like when the next shipment is coming in?" Woodson said.

"Or where they are going to house it until they are ready to ship it to the collectors."

"Bandaleri is the big fish."

"I think I need to go fishing," Liz said, slipping off the desk and adjusting her hat.

"I need to join Seth in the preserve. He dropped me off. Do you have anyone heading out that way?"

The room erupted, "Sheriff, there's been another arrow shooting."

# Chapter Fifty-Four

Sirens were screaming down the road. Liz approached the Eleven Mile trailhead with Sheriff Woodson and Deputy Franklin.

She spotted Seth standing with Zackery in the distance. Someone was on the ground being attended by the EMT medics.

Liz had her door open and was getting out before the car came to a stop. She ran to Seth, thankful he was not the one with the arrow in his shoulder.

"What happened?"

"Zackery and Matthew were hunting. Zackery saw some plants he could use for his class at the high school. Matthew was helping him gather them when he was hit. They saw someone running away but didn't go after them."

Liz knelt beside Matthew on the ground, "I'm so sorry, Matthew. We're going to catch this guy."

Standing, she hugged Zackery and then Seth. "This has got to stop. Did you see his face at all or get a sense of whether he was young or old, male or female, anything?"

Zackery hesitated, closing his eyes. "The shooter was tall, thin, male. I could tell from the way he ran. He wore camo with a ball cap and carried a backpack." He stopped and tried to recall something. "The backpack had a label on it: Straight Arrow Archery."

"Now, where have we seen that before?" Seth said.

"Right, chief, but how many members of that club do you think have that label?"

"But on a backpack and wear camo? Besides, this is personal now."

They waited and watched as Matthew got loaded into the ambulance for the ride to the hospital. Zackery would follow and let everyone know what was happening.

Someone else was watching. A man in an old pickup truck watched the ambulance scream past. He took a water bottle out of a backpack, took a long, cool drink, and smiled. He had taken the backpack after putting that guy's body in a dumpster. A dead man didn't need a backpack or water. He laughed. The game was "Catch Me If You Can," and he was good at it.

Seth talked to Sheriff Woodson again about locating Malcolm Fletcher. Woodson agreed to send deputies to the archery club and the university again. He would also ask the FBI what they could do to help locate Fletcher."

"I know that Fletcher is our main suspect, but what if it's not him?" Liz said as they walked back to Seth's truck.

"You're right. I have tunnel vision when it comes to Fletcher. I wish we could get our hands on him and have a talk. Get some answers. At least we'd know one way or the other. Where the hell is he hiding?"

# Chapter Fifty-Five

Headquarters in Tampa came back with a ruling that if Professor Newsom's information provided the FWC with information necessary in aiding the capture of persons engaged in the illegal trafficking of endangered orchids, all charges against him would be dropped. The deal would include caveats to be discussed.

Sheriff Woodson relayed the information to him through his attorney.

Maria Ortiz came to the station to inform her client about the decision. She had one bit of bad news for him. The university did not want the professor to return to campus.

Newsom was excited about the news that charges against him could be dropped. Less so with the news that his placement at the university was dropped. He would have to look elsewhere for employment. The professor was being released from jail but was required to wear an ankle monitor, which he strongly objected to.

"If I'm no longer under arrest, why do I have to wear this?" Newsom said, indicating the monitor."

Woodson kept his tone neutral, "It's a condition of your release. You have yet to give the FWC the name of the Airport. They can't arrest anyone if they don't know where the plane is going to land. The FWC doesn't want you skipping out on them."

"As if," the professor said. Miss. Ortiz grabbed the professor and escorted him out of the building before he could say anything else.

Seth and Liz arrived at the station only to see Professor Newsom sitting in a car, being driven away by Maria Ortiz.

"Shit," Liz swore. "We missed him. I hate that attorney of his. She is getting in the way of the information I need ." Closing her eyes and balling her fists, she growled, frustrated that she missed Newsom. "I hate that bitch of a lawyer and whoever hired her. I will find out who is behind all this and stake them out over a fire ant nest."

"You don't often swear my heart. This situation is really getting to you," Seth said.

"You know, Chief, it is. She helped someone circumvent a law to protect endangered species worldwide, and that person is now helping him avoid the punishment he deserves. I'm angry." Liz kicked at the dirt in the parking lot.

"Tell you what. Let's go patrol the campsites, and maybe we can give out some tickets for littering. Would that make you feel better?"

Liz pouted and leaned against Seth's shoulder, "Yes."

It didn't take long before Liz was able to write her first ticket.

A young couple camping at Burns Lake had empty food containers and soda bottles lying out beside the remains of a small grate.

The tent was zipped tight at eight o'clock. Liz gave the honor of waking them up to Seth.

"Florida Fish and Wildlife, we need to talk," Seth called loudly, shaking the tent poles.

A sleepy male voice inside answered, "Whoa, yeah, coming."

A disheveled head peeked out of the opening as the zipper came down. "What's going on?"

"Come on out here so we can talk," Seth demanded.

The head disappeared inside again. Hushed voices and rustling preceded the appearance of a young man and woman in their early twenties.

The woman rubbed sleep out of her eyes and looked at the officers. The man stood with his hands in his cut-off jeans as if trying to hold them up.

"What's the trouble, officers?" the man asked. Clearly, he had no clue about the mess around him.

"I'm Officer Grayson, and this is Officer Corday with the Florida Wildlife Commission. "You have a big problem with all the litter around your campsite. Do you have any idea how dangerous it is?" Seth said, toeing an empty pizza box.

"How can it be dangerous? It's just trash. Don't they pay someone to clean it up?" the man said.

Liz almost blew up, taking a breath before she exploded, calmly saying, "No, they don't pay someone to clean it up. You are supposed to clean it up. Leaving trash around attracts wildlife, including rats, raccoons, bears, and possibly even panthers. Once they become used to getting human food, they can become aggressive and need to be destroyed."

The woman began to cry when she heard that. "I didn't know. Spencer told me someone would take care of the mess for us. I'm so sorry."

Seth was already writing out the ticket. "I'll need to see your ID for the ticket."

The young man, Spencer, finally took his hands out of his pockets. "Valerie can clean it up. I don't need a ticket." He looked at his girlfriend. "Hell, I'll pay the fine. Let me get my wallet."

"No, this goes through proper channels. I need your ID."

"Look, this doesn't have to go that far. How about I make a donation to your favorite charity now? We call it even."

Seth nodded to Liz, who understood there was a problem and stepped away to call for someone from the sheriff's department to come by.

"Start cleaning up this mess now. You created it. You clean it. I can see raccoon tracks all over your campsite. You're lucky there are no bear tracks. If your camp were deeper in the preserve, your night visitor would have been a bear." Seth said.

"Valerie, help me pick up this shit," Spencer called to his girlfriend.

"Valerie is staying right here. You told her someone would

clean it up, right? Well, that someone is you," Liz shouted back.

Liz found Valerie a seat while Seth supervised a seething Spencer in clearing the campsite.

A sheriff's patrol car pulled up as Spencer tossed the last bit of trash into the bin and secured the lid.

Deputy Franklin emerged with a big grin on her face, "I might have guessed."

"Our young friend has earned himself a ticket for littering a national park and refusing to offer an ID for the ticket," Seth said.

Franklin put her hand on her gun, "Young man, in the state of Florida, it is an offense not to give a law enforcement officer identification when asked."

Spencer shoved his hands in his pockets again. "He's not law enforcement. He's a wildlife officer."

"Oh, let me educate you. Officer Grayson has all the authority of a law enforcement officer in matters dealing with the National Preserve. He can make arrests just as I can. I am only here to support him. Now, let's have that ID."

Pissed off, Spencer went into his tent and came back out with his driver's license.

Franklin took the license back to her vehicle and ran it through the system.

She came back dangling a set of handcuffs. "Our friend here is Spencer Kirkland. He has two outstanding warrants. One for drug possession with intent to sell and the other for driving under a suspended license." Franklin slapped the cuffs on and led the man to her vehicle.

Spencer glared at Seth and spat on the ground as he passed.

Valerie watched, stunned. "I can't believe I was so stupid. Coming here seemed like such an incredible adventure. Spencer made it appear great: hiking, wildlife, camping. You know, the great outdoors.

Liz and Seth helped Valerie pack up the tent and the rest of the camping gear.

"I'm sorry it turned out like this for you. Hopefully, you will return and enjoy the park with a better companion." Liz said.

"I'm going back to USF and my studies. I'm going to pass on men for a while, a long while.

# Chapter Fifty-Six

Woodson hung up the phone when he saw Seth and Liz walk in. "You're not going to like this. A camper smelled something rank in a dumpster at the Loop Road Campground. He thought it might be a dead raccoon. The camper about had a heart attack when he found a dead body inside. He called it in a few minutes ago."

"Aren't we lucky? A dead body, and the sun is barely up. Goody," Liz scowled.

Liz was on her way out the door. Woodson looked at Seth and said, "What's got her panties in a twist this morning?"

"She saw Newsom leaving with his attorney yesterday."

"Aw, shit, I know she still wants more information out of him."

"Put her in a room with him, and she'll beat it out of him if she gets the chance."

"I'll see if I can arrange it. You better catch her before she leaves you to walk to Loop Road by yourself." Woodson smiled a crooked smile as he watched Seth hurry out the door to catch up with his angry wife.

He reached the truck as Liz slammed the door and turned on the engine. "Hey, remember me?"

"Yeah, come on. Let's go see this dead body." Calmer now, she put the truck in gear and drove out of the parking lot.

The Loop Road ran to the south, closer to the Everglades. It was wilder and less used. The road was passable but often flooded

"

in heavy rain. It was not unusual to have to stop for a gator or turtle to cross the road.

A patrol car was already at the scene when they arrived. The deputy approached, looking visibly shaken and a sickly shade of green. "It's pretty bad. He's been there a while, cooking in the heat. I've called the forensic guys. The coroner is on their way," the deputy gagged at the thought. "I don't envy them."

"Where's the man who found the victim?" Seth said.

"He's sitting in my vehicle. He left his vehicle at Monument Lake and was walking the Loop."

The wind shifted, and the stench from the dumpster hit them.

Seth held his nose, and Liz crunched her face and tried not to breathe. She gagged and tried not to be sick.

"God, that's terrible. There is no way I'm looking at that." Liz said.

"I'll do it," Seth said. Taking a deep breath, he covered his mouth and nose and lifted the dumpster's lid, quickly looking inside. The body lay on top of soda cans, discarded pizza boxes, and fast-food wrappers.

He did a double take, dropped the lid, and went back to stand silently beside Liz.

She waited, seeing a puzzled look on Seth's face. "What's up, Chief?"

"Something is telling me that our decomp over there is Malcolm Fletcher."

"What?"

"Yeah, I swear. They look like the same clothes Fletcher wore when we saw him at the university."

"Then it can't be Fletcher running around shooting arrows at people in the park because he's been here in the dumpster," Liz said.

"We'll have to wait for a positive ID, but I'm pretty sure that's Fletcher."

The forensic team rolled up and took over. It wasn't an easy job getting the body out of the dumpster in the state it was in. Finally, the body was out and zipped into a black plastic bag for transport.

The coroner stopped to talk to them and the deputies, "I'll get back to you when I know something. Maybe later today or in the morning."

# Chapter Fifty-Seven

Back on Eleven Mile Road outside the Raccoon Point Oil Refinery, a scruffy man in cutoff jeans and a two-day-old beard waited.

A few men left as their shift ended. He wasn't interested in them. It wasn't their fault that they had such lousy jobs and a bastard boss like that.

When he'd tried to get his job back at the refinery, Halleran had laughed in his face. We'll see who is laughing now, the man thought.

He'd camped out in the preserve, living on what he could find. Other campers didn't miss the bits and pieces of food or drink he stole. The park rangers occasionally made him move on. Even the pesky FWC deputies questioned him.

He swatted at bugs and biting mosquitoes. He hated waiting.

The only good thing that had happened was meeting up with that young guy, Fletcher.

An ecology student on a mission to save the world, the man chuckled softly.

They got to talking about how he used his fancy crossbow to scare people who were breaking the rules in the preserve. After a while, the idea occurred to him to get back at Halleran for not hiring him when he desperately needed a job.

Fletcher even showed him how to use his crossbow. He was

surprised at how good he was with it.

He leaned against the water oak tree and looked up through the branches, which were covered with Spanish moss. A trio of snow-white egrets was perching high above him. He seemed to remember that getting shit on by a bird was supposed to be lucky and chuckled again.

The door to the refinery office opened, and Halleran stepped out into the heat.

Here was his chance. The man stood, loaded the crossbow, and emerged from his hiding place in the brush, pointing the weapon at Halleran's chest. "Halleran, remember me?"

Halleran stopped, "Don't know's I do." Afraid and with no one around to help him, all he could do was hope to talk his way out of getting killed. "If there is a problem, we can talk about it."

The oilman had only returned to work the day before and was still feeling rather fragile. He gently rubbed his chest where the arrow had almost ended his life.

"I came to you for a job a while back, and you gave me all the shit jobs. Then you fired me. I'm a combat vet. I served my country in two wars and can't get a stinking job anywhere now."

"Look, I'm sorry. I'll give you another chance. Anything you want, just put the weapon down. You can come to the office, and we can fill out the paperwork now if you want."

"It's gone too far for that," the man growled.

# Chapter Fifty-Eight

The coroner's office called later that afternoon and confirmed that it was Malcolm Fletcher's body. Seth and Liz drove out to Naples to see what else they discovered.

The forensic team had gone through Fletcher's pockets and found a slip of paper from the Straight Arrow Archery Club dated a week ago.

"That's about when we think your victim was killed," the tech said. "It's hard to pinpoint because of where he was found and the heat generated in the dumpster."

"I guess we're going to the archery club," Liz said.

Seth lifted an eyebrow and thought for a moment. "Whoa, we were undercover last time. Do we want to go as FWC deputies this time?"

"I think it'd better be official this time, guns and all. We need answers."

Forty-five minutes later, they walked into the archery club.

Karl was there and approached the deputies cautiously. "What can I do for you, officers?"

Malcolm Fletcher was in here about a week ago, right?" Seth said.

Karl tipped his head and stared at Seth and Liz. "Yeah, he was. Hey, don't I know you? I don't get many Seminoles here. I had a guy in here with this crazy female. She looked a lot like you, ma'am."

Seth thought quickly, "That was my cousin. Our fathers are twins, so we look a lot alike. My cousin likes to gamble, so he's either rolling in it or flat-broke, if you know what I mean. He's also crazy as a mud hen."

"Yeah, I kinda got that."

"Back to Malcolm Fletcher."

"Right, I remember it because he had the other guy with him. Max something. Malcolm took him out to the range and taught him how to shoot. This Max person was extremely good right from the start. He didn't say much, and I felt that Malcolm wasn't happy being with him.

The guy was wearing old, torn-up clothes and smelled like he hadn't had a bath in weeks.

Malcolm paid the range fee and bought some extra arrows.

"I watched them leave in this old rust bucket pickup truck. I haven't seen them since."

"Thanks, Karl, you have helped a lot. I'm sorry to tell you that Malcolm Fletcher is dead." Seth said.

"Shit, that's a shame. He was a damn good customer."

# Chapter Fifty-Nine

"Are you thinking what I'm thinking, Chief?" Liz asked on the way to their truck.

"Max Weller, our homeless man, is now the number one suspect in the murder of Malcolm Fletcher. If he killed Fletcher a week ago, why is he out there shooting arrows now?"

Liz was also trying to wrap her head around that. The A/C was struggling to cool the interior of the truck down.

"Fletcher was an eco-warrior. He shot arrows near people, breaking conservation laws and rules. We don't know why Weller killed Fletcher or why he has a gripe with the oil refinery." Liz said.

"Let's go to the refinery and ask Halleran if he knows Weller and find out," Seth said.

# Chapter Sixty

They parked where Eleven Mile Road ended and walked the rest of the way to the refinery. It was getting late in the afternoon, but the heat and humidity were still oppressive.

Along the way, they saw where a momma alligator had dug out a shallow pool beside one of the streams. She used her snout, claws, and tail to make a home along the bank. Later, she would build a nest high and dry. The pool would fill with water during the rainy season, providing a safe haven for the young. Frogs and other small animals would come to the pool to feed her growing brood.

Several men were leaving the refinery when they arrived. They didn't see Halleran among them.

"Is your boss Halleran still around?" Seth asked one of the men.

"We ain't seen him today. He didn't call in either," the man offered.

A couple of the others had stopped to listen. "That ain't like him. Since he got back, he's been on us pretty tight."

"So, who's in charge when he's not here?"

"Marty Kincaid, He took Sully's place. He's in the office." One of them volunteered.

Seth and Liz looked at each other. They were both thinking the same thing. Max Weller had taken Halleran.

The office was a cool respite from the heat. Marty Kincaid looked up from the report he was writing, surprised to see two

Florida Wildlife Conservation Commission (FWC) deputies standing before him.

"What can I do for you, officers? Not another leak, I hope."

"Not this time. What do you know, if anything, about a man named Max Weller? Did he work here at the refinery at any time?"

"Sure, I know him. I came over from the Texas office right after Halleran hired him. He felt sorry for him. Weller fed him a line about being a Veteran and needing a job because he was homeless and all that bullshit. I know some Vets are struggling, but Weller was a nut case from the get-go. He couldn't follow simple directions, always screwed things up. Weller was late or left early and always had an excuse.

The boss fired his ass, and Weller screamed bloody blue murder about discrimination and every other thing he could think of." Kincaid's eyes widened. "You think Weller had something to do with the boss not showing up today?"

"It's a possibility," Seth said. "Do you have Halleran's address and phone number? We'll try to contact him to make sure he's ok."

Kincaid dug through the computer files and printed them off for them. "I sure hope you find him and in one piece. I want to get back to Houston. This humidity is killing me."

Liz and Seth left and began their walk back to their truck. Both were lost in their thoughts.

Seth tried calling Halleran's number. It went straight to voicemail. He left a message asking the man to return the call as soon as possible.

"If Weller had taken Halleran, he must have used Halleran's vehicle because that's also missing. Weller was last seen driving an older model pickup truck. Let's check and see if anyone at the campground checkpoints has seen one hanging around," Seth said.

"It's getting late. Should we go by Halleran's place and check it out?" Liz asked.

"Let's let the sheriff and his boys do that. I'll give him a call and fill him in. I think we've done enough for one day."

They gave Momma Gator a wide berth on the way to their

truck. Liz told her to have a good night and not to let the bedbugs bite. Seth rolled his eyes and shook his head. "Only you would say good night to an alligator."

Reaching their truck, Seth hopped in and started the engine to get the A/C working. Liz grabbed a water bottle from the cooler and took a long drink. She handed a bottle off to Seth.

"I just had a thought."

"Should I be worried?" Seth joked.

Liz grinned, reached over, and punched his shoulder. "We haven't heard from Pat in a while. I wonder what he's been up to while we've been having all this fun?"

"I'll give him a call when we get home."

# Chapter Sixty-One

Sitting on the couch after supper, Nickosi again lying at their feet, Seth picked up his phone and punched in Agent Pat Miller's number.

He was mildly surprised when the agent answered on the first ring.

"Hey, Pat, what are you up to? We haven't heard from you in a while."

Seth put the phone on speaker so Liz could hear.

"I'm glad you called. I've been investigating the illegal orchid trafficking case. Since it's crossing state lines, the feds are interested. I tracked down Bandaleri. He's connected to many wealthy individuals in the Northeast. One of them is pretty high up in the Italian Mob."

"My guess is this guy collects exotic and rare orchids?" Liz said. She could barely contain her excitement at the news.

"Well, hello beautiful, yes, he does. He pays Bandaleri a pretty big commission to bring him the best and rarest on the planet."

"Have you arrested Bandaleri yet?" Seth asked.

"Not yet. We have planted an undercover agent who is trying to determine when and where the next shipment is scheduled to arrive. It could be any day now. The thing is, we suspect they are importing more than just orchids. Reading between the lines in their conversations, we think drugs are coming in as well. "

Liz took Seth's phone and told Pat about Professor Newsom. "The rat will not get his deal if we manage to shut down the traffickers without him," she said.

"You got that right. Newsom will do some jail time for his part in all this. I've got another call. I'll let you know when I hear something." The line disconnected.

Seth looked at Liz. "Hello, beautiful?" he said.

"Come on, it's just his way. Besides, you're the only one for me." Liz said, sliding over onto Seth's lap, running her hands through his raven-black hair, kissing the tip of his nose before devouring his lips and mouth with hers.

Coming up for breath, Seth said, "Ok, I believe you."

With Liz's legs wrapped around his waist. Seth carried her down the hall to their bedroom to finish what she started.

# Chapter Sixty-Two

S eth and Liz woke to the strident ringing of Seth's phone. He fumbled around and looked at the caller ID.

"Sheriff, This can't be good so early in the morning," he said.

He listened for a few minutes and flopped back. "The patrol found the old pickup at the Monument Lake Campgrounds. The forensics team will go over it and see what they can tell us."

Liz propped herself on her elbow, "Weller must have walked into the refinery from there. That leads to the question, did he plan to murder Halleran at the plant or take him and kill him later?"

Nickosi jumped on the bed and off again, wanting to go out. "Looks like our day has begun," Seth moaned, swinging his legs over the side.

"I'll let him out and put the coffee on while you shower," Liz said, following the big dog out of the room.

Seth's phone rang again as he poured himself a cup of coffee. It was the sheriff's office and Deputy Franklin this time.

"You're up early, Franklin," Seth said.

"And not happy about it. I went out to Halleran's address. There was a note pinned to his door by an arrow. It was a ransom demand for five million dollars, and the stopping of all drilling in the Big Cypress National Preserve or Halleran dies."

"You've got to be kidding?"

"I kid you not."

"It was signed, Eco revenger."

"He's creative. I'll give him that."

" I'll tell Liz and meet you at Woodson's office. We heard from Agent Miller and can fill him in on that at the same time."

"Great, see you there."

Liz walked into the kitchen, her wet hair still dripping with moisture. "More bad news?"

"Weller did kidnap Halleran. He's holding him for ransom. I'll fill you in on the way to the sheriff's station. I think Weller does have a few screws loose and is capable of anything."

On the way to the station, Seth was very quiet. Liz could tell his wheels were turning in his Seminole brain and not to stop the flow. Seth would tell her when he was ready.

About halfway to the station, Seth said, "We may need Pat's drone again."

# Chapter Sixty-Three

Woodson was pacing behind his desk when Liz and Seth arrived. "How are we gonna catch this nut case? The oil company may fork over a couple of million to get Halleran back but shut down the drilling. That is out of the question."

"I think that's what Weller is counting on. It gives him the excuse to kill Halleran. He's making Halleran suffer, and then he'll kill him. But it will be the oil company's fault, not his." Seth said, standing in front of a map of Collier County.

"I can't call the oil company yet because of the time difference between here and Texas," Woodson said, looking at a large clock on the wall. "Don't they have enough oil in Texas anyway?"

"I spoke with Agent Miller last night. He is already on his way here. I believe Weller has Halleran somewhere in the preserve."

"How the hell are we gonna find Weller if he's hiding somewhere in over 700,000 acres of forest and swamp?" Woodson's face was turning red with frustration. His blood pressure was ready to give him a stroke.

Liz handed him a bottle of water from the small fridge in the corner. "Take it easy. You'll give yourself a coronary at this rate. I'm sure Seth has a plan."

"We agree to his demands."

Woodson choked on the water, "Are you fucken nuts?"

"No, hold on, it's a stall. We inform Weller that the oil company is sending someone to negotiate and provide him with the money. How would he prefer to receive the money: in cash, by check, via bank transfer, or Bitcoin? That alone will confuse him for a while. We tell him the company needs time to shut down the wells."

"OK, then what?"

"We use Agent Miller's drone to locate Weller and take him out."

Woodson took another drink and paused, "You know you're one smart Indian."

"But I still have to call the oil company and tell them what's happening. They will probably want to send someone to get on my last nerve anyway."

Woodson yelled for a deputy to get him the oil company's contact information in Texas, "I want the head office in Houston. Not the regional office here in Florida. The regional office will only have to call Houston anyway." Muttering while he sat and tried to calm down, "Bunch of dumbasses drilling in the National Preserve. The oil they're getting ain't worth a shit no how." He was exhausted, and his Cracker roots were showing.

Franklin came in and handed out coffee. She passed the number for the head office of the oil company in Houston to Sheriff Woodson.

Steeling himself, Woodson punched in the number. He explained several times to several different people why he was calling, listening to elevator music in between, and rolling his eyes and clenching his jaw in frustration.

Finally, he reached a senior vice president who listened and said they would send someone out immediately to address the situation.

Woodson hung up. "What the hell does that mean? Deal with the situation?" he cried, rubbing his hands over his face.

The squad room erupted, and a deputy ran in, "Weller in on line one."

Woodson picked up the phone and put it on speaker. "Sheriff Woodson here."

"You got my message?"

"Yes. I contacted Sun Oil in Houston, and they are sending someone out immediately. They intend to meet your demands and want Nick Halleran to return safely. It will take time to gather the funds and even longer to safely arrange the oil wells closing."

"I'm not sure I believe they gave in so easily." Weller sounded skeptical.

"I was surprised myself," Woodson said. "But I talked to a senior VP, and that's what he said. We will need proof that Halleran is alive and unharmed."

"I'll send you a photo. Any funny business and Halleran dies. I know those FWC guys are listening to it. You have twenty-four hours."

Woodson took a slug of his now cold coffee. "That buys us a little time."

"We'll head to the airport and pick up Agent Miller. Let's hope the oil company rep gets here soon."

On the way out, Seth stopped to speak with Deputy Franklin, "Do you happen to know where they found Halleran's car?"

"We found Halleran's car at the Big Cypress Welcome Center. The forensics team had it towed in last night and is looking at it now."

# Chapter Sixty-Four

The Welcome Center was a small, log cabin-style structure situated on the side of SR 41, just a short distance from the Monument Lake Campgrounds. It was composed of a small gift shop and a rental shop for canoes and small boats. It also had a limited supply of camping gear.

A woman stood behind the counter, helping a young family.

"I'll be right with you, officers," the woman said. She was pleasant, with gray hair, and appeared to be in her fifties.

The young boy tugged on his father's sleeve and whispered as children do, "Is that man a Seminole?"

The father looked at the boy and Seth. "I'm sorry. We just visited the Seminole Museum on the Big Cypress Reservation.

"That's OK," Seth said, approaching the boy. "Yes, I'm a Seminole. I'm also a Florida Fish and Wildlife Deputy. My name is Deputy Grayson, and my partner is Deputy Corday."

"Wow, a real Seminole. Do you live on the reservation?" the inquisitive ten-year-old asked, embarrassing his father.

"No, I don't, but my parents do." Seth smiled at the boy.

"Come on. I'm sure the deputies have things to do," the father said, gently pulling the boy away. The mother paid for the purchases, and the family left, stealing backward glances at Seth and Liz.

The woman at the counter apologized, "I'm sorry about that.

Children don't always have a filter for the time and place for their questions."

Liz noticed her name badge, which read "Sarah," and addressed her. "Sarah, were you here two days ago, and did you happen to notice the blue Toyota parked here overnight?"

"Yes, I did. Usually, if someone plans to camp overnight, they use one of the campgrounds."

"Great, did you see the two men who left it there?"

"They came in and wanted to rent a two-person skiff. I remember them because they didn't seem to go together. One was scruffy and did all the talking. The other was dressed in clean jeans and a button-down short-sleeved shirt. The talker said they were going bird-watching. It felt odd, but I rented them the skiff, sold them a few bottles of water and some ice for a small cooler they had, and off they went down the Halfway Creek Loop."

Sarah reached around the counter to a display and grabbed one of the maps. She unfolded it and showed Seth and Liz how the narrow, twisting waterway meandered its way and joined up with the Turner River. Both waterways were only for paddling. Loop Road encircled Halfway Creek, a partially improved road that attracted adventurous sightseers.

Seth and Liz could see a problem. If things went sideways and Weller escaped, he could follow the Turner River, make his way into the Everglades, and disappear.

Folding up the map, Seth offered to pay for it, but Sarah refused, hoping they'd find who they were looking for.

Stepping outside into the heat, Seth saw the family beside their rented SUV. The father and mother were studying a map held out between them. The young boy waved timidly at Seth.

Seth waved back, smiling. He liked that kid. He wondered what it would be like to have a son of his own. Ever since his father asked him to join the tribal council, the idea of starting a family had been invading his thoughts. Moving to the Big Cypress National Preserve had brought him closer to his roots. Was it time to consider the future and pass on his heritage and culture to the next generation? What would Liz think? Maybe it was time to ask.

"Hey, Chief, you coming or not?" Liz said, wondering where Seth's mind had gone off to.

The launch area featured a mix of canoe and kayak racks, along with a couple of skiffs. It smelled of old wood and brackish water.

Standing at the end of the platform, Seth and Liz looked out over the shallow, curving creek. The view was postcard-perfect.

A snow-white egret sailed overhead against the azure sky. Tall cypress trees in the distance marked the entrance to the Everglades beyond—a place of natural beauty and immense danger.

Seth reached for Liz's hand. His mood was reflective; so many things churned in his head: the Tribal Council, protecting the preserve for future generations, his future generation.

The land in front of him had belonged to his people when no one wanted it. Now, everyone wanted to change it.

"You alright?" Liz asked, turning Seth to look into his gray-green eyes for an answer that wasn't there.

"I have a lot on my mind." Seth knew that sometimes only the Breath Giver of the Seminoles knew the answers.

# Chapter Sixty-Five

They swung by the Ft. Myers airport and picked up Agent Miller on the way to meet up with Sheriff Woodson.

The agent was waiting outside when Seth drove up. Pat swung his six-foot frame into the truck and settled on the back seat, putting the case with his drone on the seat beside him.

Addressing Liz, he said, "Hello, gorgeous." Knowing it would annoy Seth. " Hi Seth, your phone call left out a lot of details other than to bring the drone. Have you figured out where Wheller is hiding out?"

"He's off in an area circled by Loop Road. He took the Raccoon Point manager and made some crazy ransom demands. The oil company is sending someone to negotiate." Seth's tone was sarcastic.

Seth filled him in on finding Halleran's car and how they discovered that Weller had gone down Halfway Creek. They needed the drone to locate Weller before he could kill Halleran and escape into the Everglades.

"Oh, Liz, before I forget. We arrested Bandaleri in New York. Our agents discovered that he had another warehouse containing more illegal, rare plants. He also had a back room with cash and packages of yet-to-be-determined drugs. He was planning an auction for the orchids, but we surprised him.

"We got him on several CITES violations, and the Fish and

Wildlife Commission up there is having a field day working out how to proceed with the prosecution. The DEA is dealing with the drugs.

"I know you have questions you might want to ask Bandaleri. We have a tracker on Newsom if you want him brought in again for more questions."

Liz took her hat off and ran her fingers through her hair. "Yes, I have questions. We need to get Weller first. Then I'll think about Newsom and his part in the illegal orchid business. I'm glad Bandaleri has been shut down. Thanks for letting me know. I appreciate it." Her mind was torn between the tasks at hand: saving Halleran, catching Weller, and finding out where the plane was landing with the illegal orchid shipment. Another thought hit her hard. Would there be any more shipments with Bandaleri's arrest? Would Newsom continue without him? Suddenly, she had more questions than answers. Her stomach rolled.

# Chapter Sixty-Six

Sheriff Woodson was in his office, pacing around his desk with his phone. He was wearing a track on the floor. His face was an angry shade of red, and his eyes rolled up to the ceiling. He nodded, breathed out, "Yes, sir. I understand. Of course, sir. I will, sir." He waved to the arriving officers, motioning for them to come in. He ended the call and slumped down in his chair.

"That was the Lt. Governor. The governor is not happy that an employee of the oil company has been abducted. He heard about it on CNN, of all places. How the hell did the news services find out?"

Pat sat in one of the chairs across from the sheriff, who was fuming. "It was bound to get out. People talk. However, I haven't seen any reporters or news vans anywhere." Pat sat a bit straighter. "I wonder if Weller could have told the news outlets. It's just something he would do."

Seth stood looking at a map of the preserve. "We have to get organized and go in after Weller, bringing Halleran out safely before this escalates."

"Agreed," Woodson said. He went to the door and shouted. "Get every deputy on or off duty to the Welcome Center as soon as possible."

Phones and radios buzzed and crackled as deputies were called in off the road and from their homes. The Collier County Sheriff's Office was not a large force, but the parking lot at the

Welcome Center soon reached capacity. Sheriff's vehicles mixed in with personal pickup trucks, sedans, and jeeps. Some were towing airboats and other fishing boats.

Sheriff Woodson, Seth, Liz, and Agent Miller stood on the raised porch to address the deputies. It was already mid-afternoon. It's not an ideal time to start such an operation. They had a couple hours of light left to get the job done or risk Weller escaping into the Everglades.

Seth laid out the plan to place several deputies along Loop Road and SR 41 to cut off Weller's escape.

The drone would be used to locate Weller somewhere in the Halfway Creek area.

"We can't use OTVs or anything with a motor that would alert Weller to our presence. Once we locate Weller, Liz and I will go in with Sheriff Woodson and Deputy Franklin. We need to protect Halleran.

"The rest of you will fan out along the creek and the Turner River to be our backup. Do not let Weller get past you if we miss him.

"Remember, alligators and snakes are out there, too, so be careful. Be aware of your surroundings."

Woodson took off his broad-brimmed hat and wiped his forehead with a handkerchief. "Take care out there. Let's go catch us, this bastard."

Woodson stepped down and deployed his men to their positions.

Pat got his drone ready to fly while Liz and Seth watched. Soon, the drone was airborne. They watched it as it rose high overhead, sending images back to the computer.

"It looks so magical, so peaceful out there," Liz said.

"Right, who would know that a nutcase holding a man's life in his hands was hiding out there," Seth said. He was watching the deputies in flack vests risking their lives to save a man they had never met.

Woodson came to stand beside them with a man in a handlebar mustache. "Deputies, this is Joe Romario from the Houston office.

He is here to negotiate with Max Weller when we locate him."

Pat's hands were busy with the drone controls. "I'd shake hands, but as you can see, I'm busy here. I'm Federal Agent Pat Miller."

"Yes, I can see that. What are you trying to do?"

Pat thought it was apparent and smiled, "I'm using the drone to locate our fugitive, Max Weller. He's in a pretty inaccessible area. We can't send anyone in unless we can narrow down where he is."

Woodson introduced Seth and Liz. Romario wondered why fish and wildlife were involved in the matter.

Seth bristled, "Anything that happens in the preserve is our business."

"I don't mean to step on anyone's toes, but getting our man out safely is my priority," the oil man replied.

"Just how do you intend to negotiate with Weller?" Liz asked. "He's out there, and you're here."

"Get him on the phone, of course."

"He's out in the middle of nowhere. We don't even know if he has a phone. You will have to go to him." Liz said.

Romario looked down at his freshly pressed khaki pants and his polished leather boots, "You have got to be kidding me," he said, grimacing at the thought.

Liz hid behind Seth to stifle a laugh. She knew this guy had stepped straight from the boardroom and had never worked an oil rig in his life.

Woodson offered Romario a pair of rubber work boots from the back of his patrol car. They were close enough in size, covered in mud, and smelled like something had died inside.

Romario cringed as he put them on, and it looked like he would lose his lunch.

Pat shouted, "I got them. They are where Halfway Creek makes the turn towards the Turner River."

Looking at the map spread out over Woodson's vehicle. It was going to be a strenuous half-hour paddle to get there.

Liz turned to Seth, "You ready, chief?"

"I'm ready. You coming, Romario?"

"I guess I have, too." A reluctant Joe Romario stepped into a canoe, holding tight to the sides as Liz and Seth paddled down Halfway Creek.

# Chapter Sixty-Seven

After a few minutes, Romario began to relax. "It's not Texas, but it sure is amazing out here," he said as he watched a flock of white ibis fly overhead to their roost.

"We're almost there," Seth whispered. The canoe rocked as he swung over the side, followed by Liz.

Romario clung to the sides, his knuckles white, afraid to try and get out. Liz and Seth steadied the canoe. "You just stay low and ease yourself over the side one leg at a time like we did."

The oilman took a breath and put one leg over the side and then the other. He was up to his knees in muddy water and grass.

Seth motioned for them to keep low and keep going. "I can see a tent up ahead."

Moving closer, they saw Halleran sitting outside the tent, his head hanging down and a bottle of water in his zip-tied hands. Weller came out of the tent and looked around, almost as if he sensed something was up.

Weller nudged Halleran with his foot and said something to him. Halleran looked up and around, expecting to see something that wasn't there.

Weller took a bottle of water from a cooler and wandered away. He stretched his arms above his head and rolled his shoulders before placing his hands on his hips and looking out into the distance. Alligators lay on the banks of the creek, catching the last warm rays from the setting sun.

Seth crept closer, hoping Weller would not spot any of the deputies. He threw clumps of weed and dirt at Halleran to get his attention. It took several tosses before one landed in Halleran's lap, and the man looked up.

Seth put his finger to his lip, telling him to be quiet and to come to him.

Halleran looked around to see where Weller was before moving.

His captor had his back to him, relieving himself in the slow-moving water they were camped beside. Finally, Halleran moved crab-like to Seth.

Liz pushed the man towards Romario, "Get him to the canoe and stay there."

Weller came back and saw Halleran missing, "What the hell?" he shouted. "There's nowhere to run, Halleran."

That's when Seth stood, " You've got that a bit wrong there, Weller."

"Fuck, not you again," Weller said, spitting venom. "Where's Halleran?"

"Oh, he's safe. It's time for you to come in." Seth said.

Weller looked defeated, "It was a good try." Then he lifted his head, spat on the ground, and looked Seth in the eyes. "Except for you. It had to be you to figure it out. You and that bitch of yours."

Seth called for Liz. "I want you to take Halleran and Romario back to Sheriff Woodson in the canoe. I'll take our friend here in the skiff and meet you there. We can come out tomorrow and clean up the site."

Liz was unhappy about leaving Seth with Weller, but there was no way all five would fit in the canoe or the skiff.

Luckily, Halleran knew how to paddle, and they were on their way, stroking upstream. Liz watched as Weller and Seth stood beside the skiff before a twist in the creek took them out of her line of vision.

Weller saw Liz's canoe disappear around the bend and seized the moment. He shoved Seth hard, pushing him into the water, and jumped into the skiff. Grabbing a paddle, he used it to push himself away from the bank and into the main flow heading south to the Turner River. And he hoped for the Everglades and freedom.

Seth came up sputtering and ducked in time to avoid being hit by the paddle aimed at his head. Weller tried to swing it again. This time, Seth grabbed the paddle and pulled with all his strength.

Weller was unbalanced and flew out of the skiff, landing several feet away from Seth.

Seth heard another great splash, followed by another, before he heard, "Oh God, no, help." Weller screamed in terror and then in agony.

Two angry alligators were tearing and ripping at Weller's body.

Seth closed his eyes. But the image stayed with him.

There was nothing he could do to save him. It was too late.

# Chapter Sixty-Eight

Liz, Sheriff Woodson, and Deputy Franklin watched Seth pull the skiff into the wooden dock alone.

"What the hell did you do with Weller?" Woodson shouted.

Seth lifted his hat and ran his fingers over the still bleeding deep cut to his head. He showed the bloody results of his encounter with Weller to the sheriff.

Liz rushed to his side to examine the wound, "You'll need a few stitches in that."

Franklin brought over a first aid kit and made Seth sit down so she could play doctor.

"Never mind all that. He'll live." Woodson asked, "Is Weller still out there somewhere or on his way to the Everglades?"

"He's out there alright." Seth winced when Franklin applied some antiseptic. "Two alligators took him down right in front of me. They have him stuffed in their holes in the banks or under a log until he softens enough to tear some chunks off for dinner. You want to go after him, be my guest."

A young deputy standing nearby heard the description and quickly lost his lunch in a trash can.

"Let's take you to the emergency room and get you stitched up," Pat suggested. "Reports can wait until tomorrow."

Woodson stomped around but eventually calmed down. He dismissed his deputies, thanking everyone.

Joe Romario and Nick Halleran sat on the tailgate of Seth's truck.

Sarah from the welcome center brought them cold soft drinks, sandwiches, and some cream for Halleran's insect bites. The man was covered in bites and miserable from a lack of proper food and cover for two days.

Halleran stood, a bit wobbly, as Liz, Seth, and Pat approached.

"I wanted to thank all of you for what you did. That guy Weller was crazy. The longer we were out there, the worse he got. He was spouting stuff about saving us from ourselves and how humanity was destroying the planet. That kinda thing."

"We ran into him before and figured him to be a lonely, homeless person. Unfortunately, sometimes they have worn out their welcome everywhere else due to circumstances we are unaware of. Veterans have PTSD. Some have drug issues or mental disorders. You never know." Seth said.

"Thanks for the boat trip," Romario said. "I like both feet on solid ground, but it is a fantastic sight to see out there. I'm heading back to Texas. The only alligators I like are the kind I find on my boots," looking down at the muddy rubber boots on his feet. "I'll have to trade these back to the sheriff before he takes off with mine," Romario said, hopping down from the tailgate.

Halleran followed his boss, thanking the officers and deputies again as he made his way.

Looking back, he watched Seth swing into their truck with Liz and Pat. He owed his life to them. All he wanted now was a hot shower, a bottle of whiskey, a clean bed, and to sleep for a week.

Liz leaned her head against the headrest. She was tired and suddenly thought, "Why am I letting you drive? You could have a concussion."

Pat sat upright, "Yeah, Liz is right. Pull over. I'll drive. You're injured."

He threw his hat across the cab at them. "I'm fine. We're five minutes from the emergency room. I'll get it fixed up, and you two can toss for whoever drives home. And don't either of you tell my mom about any of this, or I'll scalp you both."

# Chapter Sixty-Nine

Seth had a pounding headache by the time they got to his house. He'd had x-rays, and there were no signs of concussion. The doctor had put in ten stitches and handed Liz a pamphlet of instructions on things to look out for, just in case.

Nickosi jumped all over Seth and Liz but reserved most of his enthusiasm for Pat.

"Yes, I love you too," Pat said, rubbing the big dog behind the ears. Nickosi was in heaven again, rolling onto his back for a belly rub.

Seth lay on the couch, and Liz handed him the pain pills the doctor had prescribed. He was going over things in his mind and wishing he had been able to bring Weller back alive. The sight of Weller being torn apart by the alligators refused to leave him. No matter what a person had done, he didn't deserve that fate.

"I'm afraid there's not much for supper except cold ham and some bread for sandwiches," Liz said, looking into the fridge. "We should have stopped and picked something up, but I wasn't thinking." All she had been thinking about was getting Seth home.

"Don't worry about it. Let me look," Pat said, moving Liz aside. "You go sit with the injured hero, and I'll rustle something up."

Liz went to sit with Seth, cradling his head in her lap. She tried to ignore the banging of pans and the rattling of dishes from the kitchen. She wasn't all that hungry anyway.

Nickosi nudged Liz as Pat called, "Dinner is served."

The table was set, and there were even a few wildflowers in a small vase.

"Have a seat. Would you like coffee or iced tea?" Pat asked.

Seth didn't know what was happening but asked for iced tea. He was getting foggy from the painkiller.

"I found the ham, some eggs, cheese, and bread. So, we have omelets and toast. I fed Nickosi his dinner." Pat served everyone and dug in, realizing they had not eaten all day.

The doctor said to wake Seth every couple of hours. He didn't suspect a concussion but wanted to be sure.

After supper, Liz tucked Seth in bed and helped Pat clean up the kitchen. She got out some bedding for Pat to sleep on the couch.

"I wish we had a guest room to put you in," Liz said.

"I've slept in worse places. The couch will be just fine."

"I want to thank you for putting supper together for us tonight. I was so worried about Seth that I couldn't think straight. Every time he gets hurt or injured, I think I might lose him. FWC officers do get killed on the job. Not often, but it does happen."

"Seth is made of strong stuff. He's not going anywhere."

Pat wanted to reach out, embrace Liz, hold her, and comfort her. But knew he would not be able to stop there. Some part of him was in love with her, yet he was loyal to Seth's friendship and would not allow himself to cross that line. He turned and played with the sheets and blankets.

"It's been a long day. You'd better try to get some sleep. Remember, you have to check on Seth during the night," He said with his back to her.

"Right. Thanks again. See you in the morning. Can you let Nickosi out before you shut out the light?"

"Sure, I'll take care of him."

Pat sat on the couch when Liz had left. Nickosi laid his head in his lap. "Looks like it's you and me tonight. Come on, I'll let you out one last time. Then it's bedtime for both of us."

# Chapter Seventy

Woodson was in a happy mood when Seth, Liz, and Pat arrived at the Station.

"The higher-ups are all pleased that Weller will not be harassing the oil company or any other park visitors again. It would have been better if he could have been brought in peacefully, but things happen," the sheriff said.

"Is Halleran back at work at the plant?" Seth asked.

"Romario took him back to Houston for some R&R. He'll be replaced in a few days with someone new. His boss was not pleased that one of his men was suspected of killing a federal agent. Another was kidnapped and held for ransom. Romario was not a happy camper. Those oil rigs are not bringing in all that much profit." Woodson went and sat behind his desk with a heavy sigh.

"Well, at least things can get back to normal now. My deputies can go about writing traffic tickets, and you all can go out and arrest poachers or whatever it is you do."

Liz bristled at being dismissed so easily. "We still have one big issue to discuss."

"What's that?" Looking at Liz and hunching his shoulders, turning his hands palms up. He didn't have a clue what she was talking about. He had been so preoccupied with Weller everything else had slipped his mind.

"The illegal trafficking of endangered orchids. I need to find

the airport the traffickers are using. I know it's around here somewhere," Liz said.

"Hold on," Pat said, jumping in. "Remember I told you that
we had arrested Bandaleri in New York."

"Yes, go on," Liz said, her hands on her hips waiting.

"He's willing to make a deal and give up the airport's name.
He also said that Newsom has gone into business for himself."

"You mean that little bastard is still dealing in illegal orchids?"

"That's right. How would you like to catch the professor
red-handed accepting a shipment at the airport and slap the cuffs
on the professor yourself?"

"Oh, I'd love that. I'd love it even better if that slimy lawyer
of his were also involved."

"Bandaleri is going to make it happen in exchange for a
reduced sentence. I want to send him away for a very long time, but
breaking the CITIES regulations doesn't carry much in sentencing.
It's usually a fine and a warning. In Bandaleri's case, he's looking
at ten years and several thousand dollars in fines. He's trying to
bargain his way out of most of it. He'll have to bargain with the
DEA on the drug charges."

"I don't like the idea of Bandaleri getting away with anything,
but if we can stop Newsom, it's worth it."

"Great, I'll let my people know. Now we sit back and wait."

Sitting back and waiting was not one of Liz's strong points.
She wondered how long it would take to get things organized.

"We better go. The last few days have been crazy. There are
reports to write and send in." Seth said, reminding everyone that
jobs were waiting to be done.

"We'll check in when we hear anything from New York," Pat said.

Pat stopped at Deputy Franklin's desk on the way out and
quietly chatted. Franklin lit up, smiled, and laughed like a giddy
schoolgirl.

Liz poked Seth in the ribs, "She's blushing. I bet Pat will have a
date tonight. Let's go. I'm not feeling so hot. Maybe I caught a bug."

# Chapter Seventy-One

Seth jokingly quizzed Pat in the truck on his relationship with Deputy Franklin the next morning. "Do I need to be worried about you and Franklin?"

"Naw, she's a sweet kid, but it's nothing serious."

"I hope she knows that," Seth said.

They pulled into a large grocery store and split up. Seth and Liz stocked up on meat, vegetables, and dog food. Pat headed for the beer aisle and a couple of other items.

Arriving home and unpacking the groceries, Seth said, "Hey, you two, how about we throw those steaks on the grill for supper? Liz, can you put together a salad for us? I'm starving."

Liz didn't feel much like eating but cleaned up three ears of corn and set out a couple potatoes to bake. She was sure she had a stomach bug she couldn't seem to shake. Just thinking of eating turned her stomach.

They discussed the day's events, and both Seth and Liz quizzed Pat on his intentions regarding Deputy Franklin. It was all lighthearted, and he finally said he was going out to meet Franklin.

"Don't wait up," the agent said as he walked out the door.

"I hope Pat knows what he's doing with Janice," Liz said. She was cuddled next to Seth on the couch with Nickosi at their feet.

"I'm sure he knows," Seth laughed.

"That's not what I'm talking about. Janice could get her heart broken. She might think it's more than a fling, you know."

"Oh God, I hadn't thought of that."

"We'll just have to be here and pick up the pieces when he moves on to someone else."

# Chapter Seventy-Two

Pat was out all night and called them from the sheriff's office the following morning to say he was ok and tracking down Newsom and his lawyer.

He told them he received a call from his office in New York. Bandaleri was singing like a canary, naming names, and finally gave up the airport's name.

He told them the airport was the Dade-Collier training airport. It was 48 miles from Marco Island and just six miles north of the boundary of Everglades National Park.

There was only one runway, and it was unmanned. It made perfect sense. A plane can land, unload, and take off, but no one would know.

"As soon as we get Newsom in here, I'll let you know."

"Thanks, Pat. We're going to be out patrolling. See you later." Seth said, ending the call.

"Looks like you're finally going to get your traffickers," Seth said.

"I can't wait to catch Newsom. I know it's going to pop up somewhere else. Illegal trafficking of plants and animals will never truly stop, but it's wrong and part of why I do what I do."

"I'm right there with you, sweetheart," Seth said, reaching out to take her hand. He looked over at her. She looked a little pale this morning and had said she thought she had a stomach bug.

Seth wanted her to take it easy and stay home, but she shrugged it off and refused.

# Chapter Seventy-Three

Their first stop was Bear Island Campground. Access to the primitive campground was a twenty-mile gravel secondary road. Campers were required to bring their own water and remove any trash.

Only those dedicated to roughing it stayed at the primitive campsites. The trade-off was the peace and quiet, the ability to hike the trails, and seeing nature as it was meant to be.

Seth and Liz walked among the tents, speaking to campers and reminding them to keep all food secure and not leave it out to attract bears or other animals.

A man with two young boys stopped them, "Hey, officers. I heard a man got taken by an alligator over by Loop Road the other day. Is that true?" The man had a New York accent, and the boys stood close to the man's sides.

"Yes, that did happen, but there is no danger of alligators around here. You must remember that any body of water in Florida could have an alligator. At this campsite, you have to watch for snakes, bears, raccoons, and the occasional possum." Seth said.

"I'm from New York. My wife took the girls to the beach, and I thought it would be fun to take the boys camping. We hiked the trail yesterday, and the boys loved it. Didn't you boys?"

The older boy, about twelve, said, "Yeah, it's ok." It was obvious the boy was less than enthused.

Liz raised her eyes and asked the younger one, "What did you think?"

"I like it. We don't get to do stuff like this at home. I saw lizards, big birds, and animal tracks. There was this stuff hanging from the trees. Dad said it was Spanish Moss."

Liz was pleased to see a child enjoying the outdoors. She guessed his age to be about ten.

She knelt in the rough sand, drew some tracks with her fingers, and had him guess what they were. They were all laughing, and the boy was thoroughly enjoying it. The last tracks she drew were those of a panther.

"Oh, I saw those by a stream we jumped over. There were big ones and small ones together."

"You are one lucky boy. Those belong to a mother panther and her cub."

"Wow, dad, did you hear that, panther tracks."

The father looked alarmed. "Should I be worried? These panthers don't attack or anything."

Seth put his hand on Liz's shoulder. "You have nothing to worry about—panthers like to stay well away from humans.

"It was nice meeting you. We have to check other campsites. Enjoy your stay."

Liz and Seth resumed their tour of Bear Island Campsite. Most of the campers complied with the rules. Only a couple had to be reminded about not leaving food out and taking away their trash.

Seth checked the time and decided they needed to make their stop at Monument Lake short. Talking to the New York family had taken up more time than planned.

This campground was situated just off the highway, close to the Oasis Visitor Center, Miccosukee Cultural Center, Shark Valley, and Clyde Butcher's Art Gallery.

There is no electricity for RVs or tents. It does have showers and outdoor grills. It was a great site for easy access to hunting and fishing within the park.

The RVs ranged from small pop-up pull-alongs to big

forty-footers that were more like homes.

Seth pulled his truck in and looked at the RVs and tents scattered around the lake. "Let's walk the lake. Grab a couple bottles of water. It's getting hot out there."

Getting out of the truck, the heat hit them like a wave from an oven. Liz held the cold water to her forehead.

Seth looked at her, "You ok? You looked pale there for a minute."

"Yeah, It was just the change from the cool of the truck to heat. It caught me off guard." Liz took a long drink of water and felt better.

They walked around the lake, talking to campers and checking fishing licenses. They spoke to a couple of hunters and checked for gun and hunting licenses.

Only one had an out-of-date hunting license.

"Mr. Jenson, I'm afraid your license is out of date. It expired last year." Seth said.

The man, gray-haired about seventy, grabbed it back and looked at it. "Well, I'll be damned. I was hunting with it in New Hampshire all winter. I guess I was damn lucky. I hoped to get one of those wild pigs you have down here."

"You can renew it right now online if you want to. We can wait, and then you will be ready to go."

The man looked at the outdated license and shook his head in disapproval. "I don't know about that. I'm not too good with that online stuff."

Liz came up to the man and said. "You get your phone, and I'll walk you through it."

Mr. Jensen took out his phone, and with Liz's help, he renewed his hunting license online.

"Thank you, officers. I appreciate the help."

"Word of warning, be careful out there. Those feral hogs can be dangerous. Keep your phone on you in case you get into trouble." Seth said.

They finished the walk around the lake and returned to the truck. Seth swung in and started the engine. Liz put her face close to the air vent to feel the cool air. "I must be getting old. I can't take the heat like I used to." She said with a slight laugh at herself, trying to make a joke out of it, but she worried she might be coming down with something.

"It's a little warmer and more humid down here than it was in Sarasota," Seth said. He had never noticed the heat getting to Liz before. The last few days, his gun-ho wife had been lacking her usual spark. Maybe it was only a stomach bug or something.

"That must be it," Liz answered, holding another cold bottle of water against her face.

Seth's phone rang as he turned on to SR 41. The caller ID read Agent Miller.

"Hi, Pat. What's up."

"We have Newsom on the way in. I got a judge to sign off on a tap on his phone and a tracker for his car."

"What excuse did you use for getting him to come in?"

"I told him that Bandaleri had given us all the information we needed and that he told us he coerced the professor into working for him. We are removing the ankle monitor. He couldn't wait to come in."

"We are on the way. It should take us twenty minutes." Seth said.

"Tell Liz we are about to set the hook and reel in her traffickers."

# Chapter Seventy-Four

"You mean I'm free to go?" Newsom said, not quite believing the officers.

"Yup, free as a bird. Bandaleri exonerated you. He said he blackmailed you into helping him." Pat disabled the tracker around Newsom's ankle and removed it.

What Newsom didn't know was that his phone calls were being traced and a tracker had been placed on his phone. The officers would be aware of every move the professor made.

Liz watched Newsom hurry from the building, jump in his car, and quickly call someone on his phone.

She had to laugh as she saw the computer tech call up Newsom's phone on the screen and listen in to the conversation. He was talking to his attorney.

The professor was bragging about how he got off scot-free and was going to be able to do business again. The attorney cautioned him not to be foolish. He claimed he knew what he was doing and disconnected.

"I told you I can't know what you are planning to do," His attorney, Ms. Ortiz, said. She was angry he had called her. Bandaleri was enough of a problem up in New York. The people who employed her were not happy that their operation was being disrupted. Of course, she would report back to them. Newsom was an idiot and would be dealt with in time.

# Chapter Seventy-Five

The officers were gathered around the conference room table. Several deputies stood listening to what was being said.

Coffee cups and donut boxes littered the table, along with the printouts of Newsom's recent conversations.

The professor had been talking to someone in Columbia about making a delivery.

Agent Miller asked, "I'm wondering. What if something other than illegal orchids is coming into the country in those shipments?"

"Now that you mention it, why is he talking to Columbia? Why not Belize or somewhere in Mexico or Central America." Seth said. "And who paid for that fancy lawyer of his? Ms. Ortiz showed up out of nowhere." Sheriff Woodson added.

"Liz and I have been out to the airport. There is minimal cover out there." Seth spread out a map showing the airport. There is an administration building, but nothing else."

Liz was very quiet, looking at the map and reading through the research she had pulled up on the airport.

"Chief, the airport is used for car rallies and racing, right?"

"What if we had some cars out there drag racing on the runway as the plane is landing? Of course, we would have to get out of the way and protest.

"The drivers would stand by their cars, watching the plane unload, and then jump in and arrest Newsom and the whole crew."

Seth kissed her in front of everyone, "My wife is a genius."

Pat tilted his head, thinking. Woodson tried to picture how it would play out.

They all agreed it would work. Now, to find the right cars and drivers.

Woodson went down the roster of deputies, finding those with access to cars that fit the scenario and were willing to participate. He cautioned them that it could be dangerous both for their vehicles and themselves. The Sheriff had ten deputies volunteering for the assignment.

"If Agent Miller is right and a Columbian cartel is involved, we may need some extra support ready to lend a hand."

"Liz gave me an idea about that," Seth said.

# Chapter Seventy-Six

Liz and Seth were on Eleven Mile Road checking OTV registrations when they got the call from Pat.

They had just stopped two teenagers from riding an unregistered off-road vehicle (OTV) too fast in the preserve. It was not only against the rules, but it was also dangerous. The teens tried to plead ignorance of the rules, but that didn't stop them from getting a ticket.

Seth was about to have them call their parents when his phone rang.

Agent Miller's name was on the called ID.

"Newsom's been a busy boy." The agent said when Seth answered. "The plane lands at three o'clock this afternoon. It doesn't give us much time to get our guys situated. Woodson needs to start calling his deputies to get their asses out there. We have about four hours to get ready."

"We'll be there." Seth hung up

The teens had waited, unsure of what to do. Seth handed them the ticket and told them to leave the preserve and not return until the OTV was registered.

Liz watched the kids drive slowly back down the trail, looking back over their shoulders to see if the officers were watching.

"You wanna bet as soon as they make the curve, they'll step on the gas."

"I don't doubt it. We better get a move on. We don't want to be late to the party."

# Chapter Seventy-Seven

The air reverberated with the sound of cars racing on the airport runway. Heat rose in waves from the ground like a dancing curtain. Storm clouds gathered in the east as the shore breeze met the inland humidity.

Agent Miller scanned the sky to the south, watching for the plane. The officers also had to be on the lookout for Newsom. He could show up at any moment. They were known to the professor, and it would disrupt the entire operation if they were spotted.

Liz watched the deputies as they sped by, wishing she could be out there with them.

Pat broke her out of her reverie. "Here comes Newsom."

The Professor's SUV entered and slowed when he saw the racers. He then sped up and stopped in the middle of the racers.

"Who's in charge here? There's a plane landing here in a few minutes," Newsom shouted.

One of the young deputies, Deputy Reed, who had been coached on what to say, stepped up. "Keep your hair on, old man. You only have to ask. We'll be happy to get out of the way and let your plane land."

He turned to the rest of the deputies. "Come on. Let's move out of the way. The man has business to do."

The deputies moved their cars to form a line facing the runway.

Pat pointed to the southern sky. A plane had its landing gear down and was making its approach.

# Chapter Seventy-Eight

The tires screeched as the plane came to a halt on the tarmac. It was a twin-engine Beechcraft Baron jet. Perfect for getting in and out of the small airport.

Newsom drove his SUV up to the side of the plane to accept his delivery. He jumped out of his vehicle, happily rubbing his hands together.

The cargo door opened, and the loading ramp was lowered. Newsom greeted a dark-skinned man who emerged. The man was of average height, wearing a white button-down shirt with the sleeves rolled up and a shoulder holster with a formidable gun.

Seeing the gun made Newsom pause, but he carried on, "You have my orchids?" Newsom said, trying to look past the man.

"Yes, professor, I have your orchids," the man sneered in a heavy Columbian accent. "I have the other packages for you as well. You know the deal."

"I only want the orchids." The professor sputtered.

"You can't have one without the other. Someone will collect the other packages. Do not worry." The man stepped closer and tapped Newsom, not too gently, on the side of his face.

Newsom raised his hand to his face, which was turning red from embarrassment and anger.

Two men began unloading boxes of illegal, rare orchids from South America and Asia, placing them in the back of Newsom's car.

The last to come off the plane was a container of individually wrapped packages.

"I don't know about this," Newsom said, watching the last container being stowed in his car.

The man placed his hand on his holstered gun, "I don't see as you have a choice in the matter, professor."

The man turned and followed his men back into the plane, ready to take off.

Newsom jumped in his car to return to his warehouse. He turned his vehicle and headed for the exit.

In his rearview mirror, he saw the cars that had been racing on the runway surrounding the plane, guns drawn. He stopped when he recognized the Sheriff and the FWC officers from his earlier encounter. *Shit, this can't be happening. The Colombians will kill me. They'll think I set them up.*

He watched, fascinated, as a short gun battle took place before the pilot gave up, and the Colombians were arrested.

Newsom suddenly realized a vehicle was approaching him. Stepping on the gas, he made for the exit again, only to see it blocked by three large pickup trucks. "What the Fuck!"

Going through them was not possible. He decided to try and go around them. Newsom didn't see the steep drainage ditch on either side of the exit. Turning to avoid the pick-up trucks blocking the exit. The professor blindly drove head-on into the ditch on the right, hoping to get to the highway.

The front end hit the dirt and crumpled. Airbags exploded in Newsom's face. He was knocked out for several seconds.

He struggled to open the door and fell into the stagnant water. Standing but unsteady, his blurry vision cleared to see Officer Liz Corday standing there, smiling, dangling a pair of handcuffs.

# Chapter Seventy-Nine

Seth, Pat, and Liz watched Sheriff Woodson and his deputies load up Newsom and the Colombians into the cars and head back to the station.

Seth made a call to Isia, his cousin, thanking him for blocking the exit to the airport. "I appreciate it, cousin. Tell the others, too. We'll be out in a day or two. There's a lot of paperwork to catch up on after this one."

"Your mother has been asking when you're going to visit. You better get your ass over there. She's got one of her feelings again. She thinks somethings up." Isia laughed.

"She always thinks something's up when I don't come around. I will be there soon."

Seth disconnected, shaking his head. "We need to go see my Mom soon. She's bugging the cousins."

"I'm not going if python is on the menu," Pat said, making a face.

"Don't worry. I'll make sure there's a hamburger for you."

" I was telling Liz, there's going to be quite a fight for jurisdiction over this one," Pat said, "The sheriff is going to want Newsom as well as you guys in the FWC. I think the Sheriff has a strong case with the attempted murder of Agent Hernandez and Malcolm Fletcher. The FWC has him for importing the orchids. The Colombians pose another problem. There are the Homeland

Security boys and the Border Protection Service, not to mention the DEA and the FAA. I would not want to be around when they all start to land in Woodson's office."

"What are they going to do about the plane? They can't just leave it sitting there," Seth said.

"The FAA will have to deal with it. I can't imagine anyone coming forward to claim it. There would be way too many questions." Pat answered.

Seth put his arm around Liz's shoulder, "You ready to go home? Reports can wait until tomorrow."

"You bet. This stomach bug is kicking my butt. I'm exhausted." Liz leaned her head on Seth. She was exhausted but happy after finally stopping Newsom and his operation. The icing on her cake was bringing down a drug operation at the same time. There might even be a promotion in it for them.

# Chapter Eighty

"Hey, we have to stop and pick up some groceries. I don't think there's much to eat at our place. We don't even have anything for Nickosi," Liz said, stifling a yawn.

Seth gave Liz a shake when they reached the grocery store. She had dozed off leaning against him.

Pat took off in one direction and Seth and Liz in another. They met up, loaded with bags, and tossed them in the back, then headed off again.

"I got some steaks, potatoes, and salad makings if you want to heat up the grill," Pat said to Seth.

"Sounds great. Liz and I have ice cream and strawberries for later."

"I hope you didn't forget Nickosi." Pat had a soft spot for the big old dog.

"No, I got a bag of his food and a big bone for him to chew on. That should keep him happy." Seth laughed. "Maybe he'll get a few steak scraps thrown in, too."

Liz shucked three ears of corn to add to the feast. She was hungry as she helped prepare the supper, but looking at it on her plate turned her off. She hoped she was over that stomach bug, but apparently not. This one was hanging on for much too long.

While Seth was clearing up out back by the grill, Pat handed Liz a small bag from the pharmacy at the grocery store.

Liz took the bag and opened it, looking up at the agent with a question on her face.

Pat shrugged his shoulders, "I've got a date. I'll see you later."

# Chapter Eighty-One

Seth looked over at Liz. "Are you OK? You didn't eat much last night."

They were driving along SR41 intending to check out the Loop Road. Seth pulled into the Welcome Center and let the engine idle.

"Sweetheart, What's wrong? Tell me, please." Seth said.

A tear rolled down Liz's cheek. "I'm so sorry. I know we were going to wait, but I must have messed up somehow."

"What are you talking about?" Seth turned in his seat and took Liz's face in his hands so he could look her in the eyes. He saw the sadness and realized she thought she had somehow let him down.

"I took a test this morning."

"I'm confused. What test?"

"A pregnancy test. I'm pregnant. Oh, Seth, I'm so sorry."

Seth was stunned. How did he not know? "What. That's, that's terrific. Don't be sorry. A little ahead of schedule, but I'm going to be a dad. You're going to be a mom." His mind raced.

"We need a bigger house. I'll get the cousins to build an addition. Is it a boy or a girl? Of course, you don't know yet. I don't know yet. I don't care which."

Liz watched him stammer, wiped away the tears, and laughed.

Seth turned off the engine, quickly swung out of the truck's cab, and ran to the other side. He pulled open Liz's door and gently helped her out so he could embrace her. Seth put his hand on her stomach.

"We have a baby in there." He lifted his eyes to hers. "You are the most beautiful, fantastic person I know." Kissing her deeply for all the world to see. The few tourists in the parking lot looked at them and laughed.

"I take it you're not mad or upset?"

"Hell no. I want to tell everyone I'm going to be a dad. I want to tell my mom and dad. My Mom will go crazy. She'll be a grandma. She can finally show pictures to all the other grandmothers."

"Not yet. Please. I want to keep this between us for a while." She didn't dare tell him Agent Miller had already guessed and had given her the test. That would not be a good idea. Seth and the agent had a minor rivalry when it came to her.

"It's going to be hard not to tell my mom and dad. We're supposed to go to their house tonight. I can cancel. I can say you're sick. No, I'll say I'm sick. They'll want to come over. No, Nickosi is sick. We're taking him to the vet. How long do you want to keep this a secret?"

"Just a couple months. I need to see a doctor and have it confirmed, and so on?"

"There is no way I can stay away and lie to my parent for months. My mom will go nuts."

"Ok, we go over tonight, but we don't say a word until after I see a doctor, promise. It could be a false positive, and I have a stomach bug."

"You're pregnant with a stomach bug. Make up your mind." Seth groaned. Seth restarted the engine and watched Liz munch on a dry saltine cracker.

# Chapter Eighty-Two

"Not a word. You promised," Liz said as they stopped in front of Seth's parents' house on the Big Cypress reservation.

"I promise," Seth made the motion of locking his mouth with a key and throwing the key away.

Rowena was in the kitchen and came out to greet them. She was drying her hands on a towel but threw it aside to embrace Liz.

"Daughter of my heart. I have been thinking of you, and now I know why."

Liz looked at her mother-in-law with wide eyes, then at Seth.

Rowena called to her husband, "Andres, come in here and greet your son and his wife."

"Woman, what is your problem? You have been acting strange for days." Seth's father, Andres, said. He brought the smell of the chicken cooking on the grill outside with him.

Rowena placed her hands on Seth's, and Liz's heads closed her eyes. "Yes, the Breath Giver of the Seminoles told me something special was to come. Now I know. Liz is pregnant."

Liz and Seth were stunned. Andres looked at his wife and quickly found a seat on the couch.

"How? We only figured it out this morning," Seth said. "We were going to wait a while to tell anyone. You kinda blew that one."

Liz sat on the couch with Andres. The older man took her hand in his for support. "Rowena knows things sometimes. I gave up trying to figure her out years ago." A broad, kind smile graced his weathered face.

There was a knock at the door, and Agent Miller poked his head in, calling, "Hey there, got enough for two more?"

Pat and Janice Franklin came in hand in hand.

Introductions were made to Seth's parents, and they moved outside.

"I hope that it's not python you're cooking today," Pat joked with Andres.

"No, we have that for special occasions. Today, we have chicken." Andres laughed, lifting the grill lid to show Pat.

"Well, I think this might be a special occasion, but please, no python is necessary. Janice and I have decided to see where our relationship goes."

Seth was thrilled. He could finally relax, knowing that the agent had a girl of his own.

Liz stood beside Seth and whispered in his ear. Seth nodded, and they both looked at Pat.

"How would you like to be godfather to our baby?" Seth said.

"Are you kidding me? Yes. It would be my honor."

# Bibliography

http://www.collierresources.com/mineral-holdings-oil-fields

Kristine Gill
September 2023
https://www.gulfshorebusiness.com/conservation-groups-seeking-to-end-decades-of-drilling-in-big-cypress/

Alexandra Martinez
July 29th, 2024
https://prismreports.org/2024/07/29/miccosukee-fight-big-cypress-wilderness-designation/

NPS.govPark HomeLearn About the ParkNaturePlantsGhost Orchid
https://www.nps.gov/bicy/learn/nature/ghost-orchid.htm

The wildlife corridor
https://floridadep.gov/sites/default/files/Florida_Wildlife_Corridor_FINAL2024_1.pdf

The Miccosukee Tribe of Indians (/ˌmɪkəˈsuki/, MIH-kə-SOO-kee)[1]
A federally recognized Native American tribe in the U.S.
State of Florida. Together with the Seminole Nation of
Oklahoma and the Seminole Tribe of Florida,
it is one of three federally recognized Seminole entities.

Amy Green
April 29, 2024
https://www.wlrn.org/environment/2024-04-29/
oil-drilling-has-endured-in-the-everglades-for-decades-
now-miccosukee-tribe-has-a-plan-to-stop-it

Chad Gillis
October 2015
https://www.news-press.com/story/news/2015/09/26/
gladesmen-culture-preserved/72553872/

*Gladesman, Photo byAdam West, Newspress.com*

Amy Hinsley
March 2018
https://blog.oup.com/2018/03/
illegal-orchid-trade-implications-conservation/

Maximo Anderson
    December 2017
    https://thecitypaperbogota.com/features/
    colombias-modern-orchid-traffickers/

Greg Allen
    September 2023
    https://www.npr.org/2023/09/18/1200223578/
    with-about1-500-ghost-orchids-left-in-florida-groups-sue-
    to-list-it-as-endangere

CITIES
    https://www.fs.usda.gov/wildflowers/Rare_Plants/
    conservation/lawsandregulations.shtml

Operations and Performance Management » Airport Authority
    https://www.colliercountyfl.gov/government/trans-
    portation-management-services/airport-authority/
    immokalee-regional-airport

*Raccoon Point Oil Refinery*

# Acknowledgments

First, I would like to thank my editor, Jeanelle Havlin, for her work in perfecting this book.

My son, Michael, who helped me with the cover design, and my husband, Peter, who reads my books looking for everything the editor missed. It's a family affair.

I get encouragement from the author community—too many names to mention.

I want to thank all those who support independent authors and provide us with the opportunity to share our work with the world.

# About the Author

Brenda Spalding is a talented writer who has received several awards.

Her expertise in publishing and marketing makes her a regular guest speaker at writers' conferences and writers' groups.

The author is a past president of the National League of American Pen Women – Sarasota Branch, a member of the Sarasota Fiction Writers, Florida Authors and Publishers Association, and the Florida Writers Association, and on the board of directors for the Florida Writers Foundation.

Her company, Braden River Consulting LLC, was formed to help other authors on their creative journey.

www.bradenriverconsulting.com

www.brendamspaldingauthor.com

www.ingramcontent.com/pod-product-compliance
Lightning Source LLC
Chambersburg PA
CBHW041052310726
48978CB00011BA/523